SONG OF KAI

SONG OF KAI

Karpov Kinrade

DARING
BOOKS

www.KarpovKinrade.com

Copyright © 2016 Karpov Kinrade
Cover Art Copyright © 2015 Karpov Kinrade
~~~~~
Published by Daring Books
~~~~~
ISBN10: 1939559456
ISBN13: 9781939559456

Dedicated to our Sonoma wine-drinking, chocolate-eating writing pals: Shannon Mayer, Elizabeth Hunter, K.F. Breene and Carmen Caine.

May the wine and chocolate be with us always. And may the words never fail us.

TABLE OF CONTENTS

THE PROPOSAL

I have sung the Song of the Dead before. As Crown Princess it has been my duty to usher a handful of high ranking puremen with royal blood from this life to the next in formal ceremony. But never have I sung this song for one I loved.

I was too young to sing it for my mother. My father sang her song, though how he managed it I will never know. He must have buried his grief deep to make it through that night. And now, I must sing Kai's.

My heart is heavy as we board the private jet that will fly us from Vianney to London. Wytt and Scarlett are by my side, each quiet, lost in their own thoughts. My father is already on board. Uncle Ragathon has chosen not to come. He said he's already said his goodbyes, but I know it's because he can't bear to return to his former home with so much bitterness between him and my father.

The last time he went to London was for my mother's memorial. He loved her too much to stay away, and loves her too much still to ever return.

I grip the cold steel stair railing as I climb into the jet. Scarlett raises an eyebrow when we enter, and I know she's surprised by the opulence. I forget sometimes that she grew up a plebeian, living a life of poverty and food rations, while I dined on pheasant and duck and rich cheeses and chocolates and lived like the Queen I will someday be.

She and I had such different lives, but here we are, in the same place. We would have been sisters someday, had Kai lived. Of that I am sure. He loved her that much. She loved him too. But now, we are more than sisters by marriage. We are bound by the blood of Nephilim. She chose my life over my brother's.

I still don't know how to live with that knowledge. That it was to be me or him, and she chose me. I know she's right, that he would have hated her and himself had she chosen otherwise. And I know the choice must have killed her in some small way.

But she made me an enemy of my people, of my family.

It's only been a fortnight since that moment forever drenched in blood.

I realize I've stopped walking, blocking Wytt and Scarlett from entering. I move forward and take a seat by the window.

The interior is a cream mini-palace with lush leather swivel chairs and a fully stocked bar. Wytt wastes no time in pouring the three of us drinks. My father has already escaped to his private office, leaving the main cabin to us.

Scarlett sinks into the chair across from me and Wytt sits next to her. I know my twin is confused by me these past several days. He chalks it up to grief, to missing Kai, to shock and recovery, but when it doesn't go away, when the secrets and subterfuge remain, what will I tell him? How do I keep the fact that I'm now Nephilim from the person who knows me best in the world?

Scarlett looks at me like she knows what I'm thinking. Maybe she does. Her silver-blue eyes are kind, sympathetic, and always these days full of apology. I've forgiven her, because she is my best friend and I love her and I don't blame her for making the choice she did. But it won't stop hurting. For either of us.

Wytt smiles. It doesn't reach his purple eyes, but he's trying. "What shall we talk about for the next hour?"

Scarlett's eyes widen as she stares out the window. "It's impressive how fast this flies."

I try not to snort. She stole a military grade fighter jet and uses it as her alter ego, Nightfall. She also has her own set of wings and could fly to London faster than this. But she's always been a pilot at heart, and this jet must seem like a dream to her.

3

Wytt nods his head regally. "Nothing but the best for a lady as fair as thee."

His flirtations fall flat, and I wonder how long it will take us to get back to normal. Is there such thing anymore? Can we find a new kind of normal after all this pain?

We drink in silence, and I am surprised when my father steps out of his office and calls my name. "Corinne, I need to speak with you."

Scarlett and Wytt look up at me as I stand. Wytt raises an eyebrow. "Any idea what this is about?"

I shrug. "Not a one."

My father is sitting behind a mahogany desk when I come in. I sink into the chair facing it.

He looks tired, older than his years. He's a vibrant man, tall, muscular, fit, with long brown hair pulled back in a tie and dark purple eyes that see everything and everyone. He's always assessing, always planning and plotting. But now the skin around his eyes is puffy, and dark bruises shadow them. His face looks drawn, as if he hasn't slept in far too long.

He and Kai never got on well, but I know he loved my brother as much as any of us, no matter what Kai thought. I can't imagine losing a child and still having to run a country.

"Corinne, I wanted to speak with you privately before we land in London."

"Alright," I say cautiously. I get the sense I am not going to like what he is about to tell me.

"You're aware of the terrorist calling himself Nico Rex?"

"Yes, of course." His Latin name roughly translates to Killer of Kings, though so far he has killed no royalty. Still, he's been a problem ever since he destroyed an A-Tech factory in Sapientia.

"Good," says Varian. "Then we shall speak briefly." He clicks on his eGlass and the eScreen on the wall changes from a waterfall to a newscast.

A pert redhead stands in front of the burning remains of a building. "I'm on the scene at the A-Tech factory outside London, where famed terrorist Nico Rex has struck again, this time destroying the second largest A-Tech lab in the kingdom. At this time seven causalities have been reported by the Hospitallers, with many more injured and seeking medical treatment. Jace Whitman, new CEO of A-Tech since the death of his grandfather, was not present at the time of the bombing, and has not made a statement to press. We understand that King Varian will be returning to his kingdom shortly. Stay tuned for a debate on what this loss means for the King. With A-Tech currently bringing in the bulk of wealth for the kingdom, the destruction of this world-renowned company could spell the end of the Ravens' reign."

5

I watch in dismay as bodies are pulled from the wreckage on gurneys. "News of this will have already reached our enemies at Court," I say.

He clenches his jaw at the mention of our rivals. "Yes. The Yorks and Skys make dealings behind my back. We'll have an uprising soon. One of the lesser houses will try to overthrow us."

I sit up straighter, the regal Princess ready perform her duty. "What would you have me do?"

He drinks deeply from his goblet before answering. "Marry. Marry the Prince of Crows and gain their allegiance."

My chest tightens, feeling the control of loss over my own body. The choice of whom I wed was likely never going to be mine. I knew this, but still, I am not prepared.

I stare into my father's eyes, seeing the ghost of past deeds buried there. "You really ask this of me?"

He sighs. "I know the timing is poor, but it must be done. I agreed to the marriage proposal a few minutes ago."

"Yes, of course," I say, clenching my sweaty hands. "Who will it be? Arion, or Norin?"

"Norin." Not the Crown Prince, then. The one who pulled on my hair when we were little and together at Court.

"And when is this supposed marriage to take place?" I ask through gritted teeth.

My father at least has the decency to look moderately ashamed when he answers me. "Two days after Kai's memorial."

"What?" I stand now, anger fueling my need for movement. I fight the instinct to unleash my wings. "That's less than a fortnight."

"It was the only way they'd agree."

"They would be getting a Queen out of the bargain. Can't they wait until I'm at least out of mourning?"

"I'm sorry, Corinne. I wish there was another way."

I walk to the door leading out of his office, then turn, my hand on the polished knob. *There is another way, and I will find it.*

...

London is cold and dreary, and I smile and breathe deeply of the wet air when I step off the plane. A man in a tuxedo steps up to us. He is tall and pale with short black hair. His face is older than I remember, though it has only been a handful of months since last I saw him.

I hug the man tightly, and though he feigns offense, for he is a plebeian and our servant and I am the Crown Princess and this behavior is entirely unbecoming one such as I, I know he is happy to see me. "Princess, your car awaits," Darris says, fighting the twitch of a smile on his stern face.

"It's good to see you again, Darris," I say, handing him my bag.

He nods his head. "I am sorry for your loss."

My smile slips. It's his loss as well. He loved Kai. Darris has been our driver since we were born. He was the driver for our mother before us. He has lived at our castle and served our family for so many years, he is practically family himself. I lay a hand on his arm and squeeze gently. "He will be missed by us all."

It's all I can say if I don't want to cry. And the time for tears is not upon me yet. I shed the first of my tears the night Kai died. I will shed the rest the night I sing his song. Until then, I must be strong.

A black limousine is waiting for us, and Wytt, Scarlett, my father and I slip into the spacious seats as Darris loads our luggage into the trunk and drives us out of the airstrip and toward the castle looming in the distance, a great silhouette of sharp edges and towers mired in London fog.

The familiar cloak of home wraps around me as Darris pulls up to the front gates. I scramble out and pull Scarlett with me, linking my arm into hers. There has been too much silence. Too much sadness. Today I will show my best friend the life I grew up in, and I will only allow happy memories of my brother into my heart, and I will celebrate his life, and my life, and we will find joy and happiness again. I tell her all this, whispering into her ear as my father disappears into the castle ahead of us.

I know Scarlett is uneasy around my father. He is her enemy, and she is his. I walk the shadowed path between them, a foot in each of their worlds. Life seemed so simple not so long ago. Now it is filled with land mines.

Scarlett smiles at me and places a hand on the grey stone wall crawling with ivy. "I can feel the history here. So many stories. So many voices echoing."

I raise an eyebrow at her. "Please tell me you're not getting *another* talent when I haven't even gotten my first."

She grins. "No. Just a fanciful imagination. I must be spending too much time with Wytt."

Speak of the devil, my charming twin saunters up to us, and throws his arm around Scarlett's shoulders. "Did I hear my name, perchance, fair maiden?"

"Scarlett was just saying how you've been a bad influence on her," I tease.

He frowns, creasing his handsome face dramatically. "Pray tell, and I shall correct my behavior hence forth."

Scarlett laughs and nudges him. "I'm taking on your dramatic interpretation of the world. You've infected me with your poetry."

Wytt laughs, and this time it is a real laugh, reaching all the way to his eyes. "In that case, I shall endeavor to keep the infection going until it consumes you. For nothing is as healing to the soul and the world's soul as poetry and wonder."

The tall, carved wooden doors stand open into a high ceiling entry way with a crystal chandelier hanging over us. A thick carpet of vibrant reds and purples cushion our feet, and tapestries are hung to either side of us.

I bend to my knee and run my hand over the carpet, looking for the spot. "Remember this, Wytt?" I point to a red stain over a cream rose.

He nods. "Kai was trying to sneak glasses of wine for us all out of a party and spilled it when he tripped over the carpet."

Scarlett smiles, kneeling with me. "How old was he?"

I look up at Wytt. "He couldn't have been more than twelve? And we were so young. None of us had any business drinking wine, but he thought it would be fun. That it would make us more worldly and sophisticated."

Wytt chuckles. "The three of us tried to clean it up. Do you know how much mess three broken glasses of wine makes? We got most of it, but this stain remained."

Scarlett and I stand and we walk into the great room. A fire is burning in the fireplace, and overstuffed couches and chairs are placed throughout the room in comfortable nooks for conversation, games of chess, or reading. "Would you like a tour, Scarlett?"

She nods, and Wytt and I show her around. To the family kitchen, just off the great room, down to the ballroom and formal rooms for entertaining. There are sections of the castle for guests, for politics and social events, but the great room and the north wing are where we live. It is reserved for friends and family. For intimate and more casual relaxations.

It takes time to make our way through the castle. I introduce Scarlett to any servants we come across.

"I'm impressed you know everyone's name and life story," she says.

I shrug. "They have been in my life for years. They mean as much to me as anyone. I care not for their status or rank, only their heart." It's not a popular opinion to hold as one of the highest ranking patrician royalty in our world, even by my father, but it is what motivates me. I have spent too many hours with my brothers begging treats from the cooks in the warm, bustling kitchens, heard too many of their stories of heartache and joy, had too many scrapes and bruises mended by Granny Gertrude who dabbles in herbs when she's not baking breads for us, to see them as anything less than myself.

I pop my head into the pantry and see Jane stacking plates from dinner. "Have you seen Granny?" I ask.

She looks up, fresh-faced and young. She's Granny's actual granddaughter, but Granny adopts everyone at the castle as hers eventually. "She's in her cabin resting."

"Is she okay?" My heart beats a little faster. I'm not ready to lose more people I love.

Jane smiles kindly. "Yes, she's fine. Just getting older, as she says."

I drag Scarlett out of the castle, Wytt following. "You must meet Granny. You'll love her."

Scarlett is still too quiet, and I know she's thinking thoughts she can't share in front of Wytt. It kills me, having secrets from him. I vow to get her alone soon so we can talk. But for now, I want to see Granny, to introduce her to my friend, to find out how she's been over these last months.

We walk down a wooded path toward the cottage. She's the only servant who doesn't live in the east wing of the castle, but even the kings and queens of our kingdom don't tell Granny what to do. It makes no matter that she's a plebeian, or a zenith. She is Granny and no one messes with Granny.

"Wytt, Kai and I would visit with her every day after our tutors left," I explain as we hike the trail.

Wytt kicks a stone out of the way and nods. "She'd make us gingerbread cookies and tea and tell us stories of the old ways, of old worlds before this one, of times long past."

"I loved her stories. She'd also read our tea leaves at the end and tell our futures," I say.

Wytt laughs. "They never came true. She's a terrible soothsayer."

I frown as an old memory tugs at my mind. Something she told me many, many years ago, when I was too little to understand. "I don't know if that's true. I think they didn't come true in the timing or ways we expected it, but she spoke many truths."

My voice sounds distant and flat, as the buried memory surfaces.

I was maybe nine years old. Still too young to know much, but old enough to think I knew a great many things. Kai and Wytt were out playing in the woods, but I stayed behind to talk with Granny and help her crush the herbs for her potions and healing tonics. Even then I knew Hospitaller would be my Order. I wanted to know as many ways to heal and help others as I could.

After the herbs were stored, she made me a cup of tea and we sat in front of her fire. We talked of things I've long since forgotten, her voice a deep resonance that soothed me into daydreams and mental wanderings.

When I'd drunk the last of my tea, she grabbed it from me and studied the bottom of the cup. Her hand, always so steady, so strong, shook, and when she looked back up at me, her eyes were haunted by her visions.

"What did you see, Granny?" I asked.

I expected cautionary tales meant to keep me from getting hurt. Something like what she'd told Wytt the week prior about not climbing the rocks by the water-fall. He didn't listen of course, and ended up cutting his hand open.

So I waited, and I promised myself I would heed whatever warning she gave. I didn't want to get my hand cut open. It would keep me from my secret trainings. The trainings I'd been sworn to tell no one about.

But when she spoke, it was as if her voice was com-ing from somewhere else. Not another place so much as another time.

From the past? Or maybe the future? I couldn't tell. But her eyes glazed over and remained unfocused as she told me words that soon faded from my memory, until now.

"You will fly with the birds, my raven child, but the price will be paid in golden blood. It is as it's meant to be, but not as it should be. Not until you rise from the ashes of your former self and don the cloak of what you were destined for."

Her words meant little to me. There were no warn-ings I could heed, no places to avoid, no situations

I could change. When she gained clarity again, she hardly remembered her own words, and we went back to telling stories.

But now, her words haunt me.

I do fly with the birds.

And the price for that was paid in blood.

But what cloak must I wear now?

What am I meant to be?

What more does this strange vision want of me?

I can't find out today, not with Scarlett and Wytt here. But I must find out soon. If Granny knows more about what has happened to me, I need to know.

The smoke from her cottage's chimney is the first thing we see, its dark tendrils twisting into the windy sky heavy with clouds.

Her cottage is small, made of common wood found in abundance in our forest, but it has a magic to it that makes it special. It's not Eden Architecture, but it's something older than that, more ancient and earth focused. Her house seems to grow from the earth and has shaped itself against the great mountain it is flush against, so that the mountain makes up one of her walls.

We walk between two griffin statues that guard her front door. From the corner of my eye I could swear one of them moves, but when I look directly at it, it's as still as any statue should be.

The path to her door is cobbled and old, and some of the stones underfoot have strange symbols written on them in dark ink. At least, I hope it's ink.

I shiver as I step over one, the hair standing up on my arms and neck.

Scarlett reaches for my hand and I can tell she feels it too. What's happening?

Before we reach the door, it flies open. Granny is standing there, her long white hair flowing in waves around her shoulders. Her face looks the same. Ancient, ageless, full of wisdom. She's bent over more than the last time I saw her, leaning more heavily on her carved wooden walking stick, but her green eyes are still bright, sharp, quick.

The look she gives us is disconcerting.

But her words are even more so.

"And so it has begun, my child. I had hoped we had longer."

Wytt looks at me and frowns. He has no idea what she's talking about. He never knew of her prophesy. And he doesn't know what I've become. But Granny does. Somehow she knows Scarlett and I are Nephilim.

She invites us in and we sit in hard chairs by her fire as she bustles about in her small space for teacups and herbs. There is a fire with a cast iron pot, a table covered in flowers and herbs, a modest kitchen, a few chairs for guests and a bed in the corner where she sleeps. She'd have more space in the castle, more luxuries. My family has always treated our servants well, zenith or not, and have provided them comfortable lives. But Granny will have none of it.

She fusses about and then turns to us, empty basket in hand. "Wytt, my child, could you please fetch me some brinberries? I seem to be out and cannot finish the tea without them."

Wytt looks up in surprise. "Uh, sure? Of course."

He takes the basket from her and gives Scarlett and me a quizzical look. I shrug and shake my head like I have no idea what this odd behavior is about. When he realizes he'll get no more explanation, he exits the cottage, likely heading toward the river north of the waterfall, where the brinberry grows in abundance. It's not a common ingredient for teas, but it seems important enough to Granny right now.

Once Wytt is out of earshot, Granny turns to us both. "Now, let us do away with pretentions, child. You have been turned," she says to me, "And your friend, here, turned you. Why?"

Scarlett sucks in a surprised breath, and I lay a hand on hers. I don't want her using her abilities on Granny. I can handle this.

"She turned me to save my life. I would be dead if not."

Granny stands silently regarding us for a moment, then nods her head and sits in the chair facing us. "The tea leaves saw this."

She looks at Scarlett. "You had to choose. Between a deep love and deep friendship."

Scarlett's eyes swell with tears as she nods.

Granny places an old boney hand on hers. "You chose what fate intended. No more, no less. But you also chose what he would have wanted. I think that means more to you, does it not?"

Scarlett nods again, still unable to speak.

She stands and comes back with two cups of teas. "Drink these. Quickly, while they're still hot."

Scarlett palms the cup hesitantly. She is, from my experience, slow to trust anyone. I smile at her, and nod, and after a moment, we both drink. It tastes vile, but I gag it down. Granny grabs the cups from us the moment we drain the last drop, studying the leaves with her old eyes.

She looks at me first. "You will lead the people, but not the way you think. Against a threat, but not the one you know."

She then looks to Scarlett, her hand shaking again, like it did with mine so many years ago. "You will destroy humanity, or save it. The leaves do not know which. Only one person knows the answer to this."

Scarlett looks more pale than normal. "Who?"

Granny looks into her eyes. I know that look. It's the soul-probing look. "You. Only you know the answer, but you do not have all the truth needed to know the answer. So only your future self knows the answer."

Wytt is out of breath when he barges back into the cottage holding a basket with the berries. I suppress a grin. My twin knew he was missing something, and he hustled to come back before we could say or do anything too interesting without him.

Granny pushes the cups to the side and accepts the basket he offers. "Thank you, my boy. Now sit, warm yourself, and I will make tea and cookies."

We drink the honeyed brinberry tea and eat the cookies and talk about things that have happened since we've been gone. We tell her of our training and of Kai and his courage and of all the things she would want to know, and many she probably already knew.

It is dark when we leave, and Wytt is chattering on about his plans for the night, and do we want to join him at the local pub to impress the locals with some royal entertainment?

"Not tonight," I say, not even faking the deep yawn that escapes me. "I'm knackered."

"Bloody hell, sis. You're too young to act so old."

I laugh. "You go, have fun. I'll get Scarlett settled in her room and get some rest. Maybe we can go out tomorrow night and I'll sing."

He seems content with that potential promise, and while he shuffles off to his night out, Scarlett and I walk back to the castle.

I haven't told them about what my father has done, about the man I'm to marry, but I will have to shortly. It will be common knowledge before long.

But I want one night home without that worry at the forefront of my mind.

Scarlett is impressed with her room, and I leave her to rest, retreating to my bedroom. But I don't undress or take to bed, as I promised. Instead, I pull back a large tapestry and run my hand over the stones until I find the right one. I push it in and a secret door opens, revealing a narrow stone staircase that leads down.

I take a fairy light from my room and follow the steps for several minutes. The tunnels under the castle are dank and full of cobwebs, but I can see the small signs of life. I smile and blow the dust off a short stone ledge before depositing my offerings. A loaf of bread, a pear, a sweet honey treat, and more paper and charcoal to help him with his budding art talent. He indicated once he wanted to learn to draw like me, so we've been doing lessons.

"Pip? Are you here? I've come home."

Small feet scurry in the darkness and I feel a cool draft of air moments before the boy appears before me.

He's pale, slight, like a vision or ghost. But I know he is real. I hold out my arms and he runs into them. "It's so good to see you, Pip."

Pip doesn't speak. He never speaks, not with words, but he makes a chirping sound that I know means he's happy and he hands me his treasure. It's a small rock, but when I look closer I realize it's not just a rock. It's an uncut diamond.

He's very pleased with himself as I stare, dumb-founded at this treasure. "Pip, I can't accept this. It's worth a lot of money."

I try to hand it back to him but he pushes it back to me, frowning and grunting. He's becoming agitated. I slip the stone into my pocket and kneel to face him as he rocks back and forth moaning. "Sh…I'm sorry. I love my gift and will cherish it always. Thank you."

He finally calms and clasps my hand as we walk deeper into the tunnels. "Is my old friend here?"

Pip nods. He navigates these tunnels better than anyone. I don't know his story, but I know he's lived down here most his young life. I've tried bringing him above ground for a better life, but he just runs away and hides until I agree not to interfere. This is his life. Where he feels most secure. So I bring him food, and he brings me small treasures and we keep each other company when one of us is feeling lonely or sad.

He looks to be about seven years old but must be several years older since I've known him for at least five.

Whoever he is or however he got here, he is my secret friend and knows more of my own secrets than anyone. Only a few others know of Pip's world, but at my insistence they let him be.

We reach a second door, and Pip knows it is time to leave. With a smile, he scurries off into the darkness. This door takes more effort to push open, but I manage it, and find myself in a secret training room. It's large, with weapons lining the walls and a space in the middle for sparring. I look around for clues that it's been used since I've been gone, but all I see are cobwebs. I dust some away, and pull out my favorite training sword, twisting it around in my hand, remembering the feel of it from hours and hours of practice.

I hear him before he announces himself, but I let him watch me as I go through a few drills learned long ago.

"You're rusty," he says, his voice low and gruff.

I turn and bow to him. Then I run up to him and throw myself into a hug.

He sputters something but manages to hug me back. "That's enough, girl. Have I taught you nothing?"

"You've taught me plenty," I say.

"It is risky for you to be here," he says. "All eyes are on you these next few weeks. And you brought a very interesting friend with you."

"She doesn't know about you or our training. But I need you. Things have changed. My father…"

"I know what your father has done. And I know more about why he has done it than you."

I look up at the old man. His blue eyes are penetrating and his long white hair is pulled back. "What do you know?"

"That the Queen of Crows is prepared to align with him against the Pope if you marry her son. That there is indeed an uprising growing, but it's not the real threat. That you are a pawn in his game, and always have been."

"Then help me. Help me, Myrddin. You are the only one who can."

...

I train late into the night with Myrddin. And it isn't until the sun is rising again that my old mentor confronts me with my secret. "You have been turned."

I huff in frustration. "Am I wearing a flashing eScreen on my back announcing this to the world? First Granny, now you."

He chuckles. "That old woman sees everything, but tells nothing. Worry not about her. And worry not about me, either. I know more secrets than you know exist, and I will keep yours too. And Scarlett's."

"What? What do you know about Scarlett?"

Myrddin grins. "Did you think you were my only trainee all these years? I've trained others, though none as extensively. I found Scarlett when she was little, tracked her and her parents to their hideaway in Sky. I knew she would be needed. Granny saw that and sent me. So I went. I gave her what she needed as best I could before I was called away again. The Tribunal has been preparing the way for change for many generations. And in you and your new friends we finally have the skill, training and aptitude we need to succeed."

I shake my head. "Sometimes I worry that the Tribunal is as bad as the Orders, using me and those I love as chess pieces to fight your wars."

Myrddin shrugs. "You are not wrong, child. The difference is we are giving you a choice. And we are telling you our motivations and letting you decide the role you play. Have the Four Orders given you as much?"

"No," I admit. "But you keep secrets. You admitted as much just now."

"Yes, but they are not my secrets to tell, and they are not relevant to the choices you make. Just as I do not tell your secrets to others, I do not tell others' secrets to you. It is the way of our Tribunal. Would you have it any different?"

I sigh. "No. You know I wouldn't."

"Very well then. Are you still committed to this path?"

"Yes."

"Then we will help you now. I take it you are not keen on marrying the Prince your father has chosen?"

I glare at him. "I'm not keen on being used a pawn in a game where I don't know the rules."

"Then let us change the rules, shall we?"

I smile for the first time since this conversation began, as I allow my blue wings to unfurl in feathers of light from shoulder blades. "We shall."

JACE WHITMAN

I only get three hours of sleep before I'm awoken by a young serving girl I've never seen before. She's no older than me, with dark eyes and dark hair and olive skin. "Good morning, Princess. I am Lea. The King requests your presence for breakfast before he begins his day."

I groan and pull the thick comforter over my head. "I'll be down in five minutes."

I don't hear her leave, so I peek out. Nope. She's still standing there, awkwardly.

"Pardon me, Your Grace, but he has asked that I help you dress for breakfast."

"I can dress myself for something as simple as breakfast."

She looks down at her feet, as she tugs on her white skirt. "He says there will be a guest at breakfast and you will need to dress accordingly."

"Bloody hell." My brother's crass language is rubbing off on me, and I don't even care. But my curiosity is peaked, so I allow her to put my hair up and help button me into a morning gown of Eden Fashionables. It's a deep blue with white pearls beaded into the fabric.

When I arrive in the dining room, my father is standing with another man I don't recognize. Scarlett and Wytt aren't there, and I can only assume that means they haven't been summoned from their slumber for this breakfast meeting.

The man before me is in his twenties, with a thin, strong frame. He's tall, with blond hair and blue eyes, and he wears a dimpled smirk on his face that, for a moment, reminds me of Kai. I flinch at the comparison, then settle my face into something more neutral.

I had half worried my father would ambush me with Prince Norin, but this isn't the adult version of that child who bullied me those years ago.

"Corinne, thank you for joining us. I'd like to present Jace Whitman. Jace, this, of course, is my daughter, Corinne the Crown Princess of Sapientia."

I bow my head just a fraction, as befitting his rank and mine.

"It's a pleasure, Your Grace."

My father gestures for us to join him at the table, and we each take a seat next to him. It's too large a table for such an intimate meal, and as we dine on eggs and meat and fruits and cheese, the clash of silver against stoneware echoes throughout the room.

"I'm sorry for your loss, Mr. Whitman. I understand your grandfather recently passed, leaving you A-Tech to run."

His eyes are unreadable, but he does an admirable job of smiling gently. "Thank you, Your Grace. And please, call me Jace."

I nod. "Very well, Jace. I assume you have been raised to take over the company?"

He clears his throat, and uses a napkin to wipe his lips. "Well, not precisely. I had other interests until this recent turn of events."

"I see. Order interests?" I ask, realizing how little I know of the man who now controls much of the fate of my kingdom. "Which Order are you?"

His eyes skirt to my father, then to me. "I chose not to follow that path. It didn't suit my temperament at the time."

"You sound like my brother, Kai. He didn't want to join an Order either. He only went for Wytt and me."

Bringing up Kai throws cold water on our conversation, and we go back to eating. I tap my eGlass and type on my eWrist to do a search on Jace Whitman.

The search results are mostly filled with sensationalized accounts of his partying and playboy ways. He's with a different woman in each of the stories. They are always beautiful and unknown. This doesn't look like the kind of man equipped to take over the world's largest and most powerful technological manufacturing company, the company that first branded the term A-Tech. "Wasn't it your great-great-grandfather who originally patented the first GenMod technology?"

Jace nods. "And we still hold the patent for all the recent advances made in GenMod, as well as in zenith research and applications."

"Most of your family members have been Hospitallers, yes?"

"Yes."

"I'm surprised you didn't choose that path in preparation for your legacy."

"It's my understanding you are choosing the path of Hospitaller, yes?" he asks.

I set my glass of juice down and look at him. "Yes."

"Not Templar? Like your father? Wouldn't that be more useful for a ruler?"

"A good ruler must lead, but also heal. I do both."

"A-Tech has been run by healers too long. Maybe it's time they had someone with business sense at the helm," he says, his grin sardonic.

"And what in your resume leads you to believe you have business sense?" I ask.

My father clears his throat, a not-so-subtle hint that I should stop talking. I'm not good at hints though.

"Is it the gambling? The partying? The womanizing?" I stare directly at him, challenging him with my glare, with my words, with the truth.

He leans back in his chair, looking non-pulsed by my inquisition. "You'd be surprised the connections you make and skills you acquire living the kind of life I have. Sometimes lessons learned in the real world are more useful than those learned in ivory towers...Princess."

"Let's hope you're right, since not only the fate of this kingdom, but the fate of your own wealth, rests on your ability to live up to the claims of your ego."

Jace pushes himself back from the table and stands. "Don't worry, Princess. No one cares more about my wealth than me."

He bows just enough to not be offensive and then bows to my father. "King Varian, thank you for inviting me to breakfast. I hope we can speak again soon."

My father nods and Jace leaves the room. My father waits until the door closes behind him to frown at me. "That wasn't necessary."

"You know his background. He's not ready for this responsibility, especially with a terrorist attacking his company. What are you going to do about him?"

"I'm going to let him do his job. I'm going to help him figure out why Nico Rex is trying to sabotage all of us. And my first step will be to secure an alliance with the House of Crows."

"By selling me to the Queen's son."

"When did you get so dramatic?" he asks, his voice stern, but his eyes softening. "There's more going on than you know, Corinne."

Oh, I know. But I can't tell him what I know. What I can do is find another way to handle the situation so this marriage doesn't take place. I am not going back to Initiate Training a married woman to a man I don't even know.

I push myself out of my seat and bow my head to my father, but he grabs my arm before I can leave. "There's something else I need to speak to you about," he says.

I pause, waiting.

"We will host a ball, here at the castle. It will be your coming out to announce your engagement to the Prince and secure our alliance. It is planned for one week hence. I've informed the staff to begin preparations. You'll need to have gowns made for you and Scarlett."

"How could you possibly think the timing on this is appropriate? With Kai's Song of the Dead coming upon us, with our family in mourning, you want to have balls and weddings?"

"Corinne, more than our own happiness and whims are at stake here. If this kingdom falls into the wrong hands, so does the fate of the Orders."

I take a deep breath and try to collect myself. My father will not be swayed by adolescent anger. I must use logic. "Very well, I have a proposal. You give me until the Song of the Dead to catch the terrorist. If I haven't, I will marry the Prince willingly. But if I have, we call it off."

The King sighs. "That's not the only thing at stake here. There are things you don't understand."

I expected this response, and so I throw my final dagger at him. "It will be enough. We will make a public statement. The kingdom will know the House of Ravens was strong and decisive in ending this terrorist." I lean in closer to look at him. "And you owe me this, father. You owe me for Italy. So you will agree to this, and I will catch your terrorist."

His face pales and I almost feel bad throwing this in his face. Then I remember the true victim of that night and my heart hardens. He should be the one feeling bad.

"You're right. Very well. If you somehow manage to catch Nico Rex *before* he destroys all of A-Tech, we will call off the wedding."

I spin away and leave the room, the door clicking shut behind me.

I'm restless, edgy and unsure where to go or what do to, so I decide to call a meeting of the two closest people in my life. It's time to tell Scarlett and Wytt what's going on. At least part of it.

I should tell Scarlett everything, but I don't know how much Nightfall should know about the Tribunal.

I didn't know Myrddin had trained her as well, and I wonder why he told me that now. Does he want me to bring her in on this, or was he testing me?

I wake them both, and envy them the extra sleep they got. They join me in my sitting room a few minutes later. Scarlett is sipping LifeForce and she tosses me one. I smile, and take a deep drink. "Thank you."

Wytt rolls his eyes. "You two are addicts."

"We don't drink as much of this as you do of alcohol," I remind him. "So who's the addict?"

"Fair point," he says, shutting his mouth about our necessary energy drink. It gives my Nephilim blood the nourishment it needs, though he doesn't know that.

I fill them in on my father's plans for me, and they are as outraged as I'd hoped they'd be.

"What are you going to do?" Scarlett asks.

"Depends. Are you two willing to help?"

"Obviously," Wytt says.

Scarlett nods. "You know I have your back in all things." Her words are laced with double meaning, and I appreciate it more than I can tell her right now.

"Here's the first part of my plan."

I lay out the details. I don't tell them I don't actually have a second part of the plan, but they agree to everything I say. Now all we have to do is catch a terrorist.

A-TECH

It's a brisk morning with a fresh coat of snow covering the world. I love how life looks blanketed in white powder, so clean and unspoiled. I pull my black pea coat around me and look for my driver, but a different car pulls up. A man steps out. "Mr. Whitman sent me to drive you."

"Oh." I wasn't expecting this when I set up an appointment to take a tour of A-Tech, but I slide in. There's a note on my seat and I open it.

I'm looking forward to our visit, Princess.
~JW

I can't help but grin at this personal touch. Maybe the stories of Mr. Whitman are just that...stories made up by a drama-craving public. I did more research on him, going deeper into the stories, and something stood out to me. While there's a lot of wild speculation about Jace, he's never actually been seen doing anything untoward. It's almost like the reputation were cultivated deliberately. It makes me curious to get to know the man himself, not his reputation. Maybe I was too quick to judge.

A-Tech is situated in the outskirts of London proper, a massive building full of angel sculptures and clean lines that contrasts dramatically with the more whimsical architecture of the area.

My driver pulls up to the front, and I step out and walk up stairs and toward tall glass doors flanked by private security dressed in black uniforms with the "A" logo on their chests.

I just reach the doors when they open, and Jace is standing there, tall, blond, dressed in a suit and smiling at me. "Welcome to my world, Princess."

I return his smile. "Thank you, Jace. Please, call me Corinne. I know you must be a busy man. I appreciate you taking the time to introduce me to A-Tech."

"I admit to being surprised by your desire to tour our facility," he says as I walk with him into the building.

"As future Queen, I need to know what's going here." I look over to him, our eyes meeting for a moment. "I'm sorry about your other facilities, about the bombings and the people you lost. I'm here to help. To see if we can figure out what's going on and stop it."

He tilts his head in acknowledgement of my words but doesn't say anything as we walk across the marble floors of the large lobby. Behind the front desk a waterfall of changing colors covers one of the walls. The man working there nods to us and Mr. Whitman greets him by name, then turns to a private elevator guarded by two security personnel. He uses his thumb scan to open it and we step in.

"You've got a lot of security protocols in place," I observe.

He nods. "Clearly not enough, given the recent terrorist attacks on one of our research labs."

"It must be hard taking over such a big enterprise while in mourning, particularly with these attacks."

The elevator takes us up, and he looks at me, a somber expression on his handsome face. "We all have our crosses to bear."

Indeed we do.

"Come," he says as the elevator stops and the sleek silver door opens. "Let us put away our grief for a time and revel in the miracles of science."

I grin at his theatrical introduction and follow him into a large warehouse on the top floor. In the middle sits a sleek golden jet that bears a striking resemblance to the Night Raven Nightfall confiscated and uses for her rebel work.

"This is Golden Raven, the Night Raven 2.0," he says, with clear pride in his voice. "Faster, more responsive, with advanced cloaking technology and better tracking abilities."

"It's impressive," I say. "But doesn't everyone pretty much hate the Night Raven now?"

"It's true that ever since Nightfall stole the Night Raven in New York, the press has been hard at work lambasting it as a rebel symbol. But when the pats and nobles saw what it could do, the orders started rolling in. That's the duality of human nature isn't it? That we want what we fear. That's why we revile Zeniths while at the same time creating the GenMod technology that allows us to become like them."

Interesting. Beneath his boyish charm and good looks there's a thoughtful man. Maybe he could do something great with this legacy.

"Why do you think Nico Rex is targeting your company?" I ask.

"He is a terrorist who wants to cripple progress," Jace says. "Since A-Tech is at the forefront of that progress, we make an appealing target."

I lay a hand on its wing and imagine flying, when Jace taps his eGlass and frowns.

"What's wrong?" I ask.

He shakes his head. "Maybe nothing. Care to see my office?"

It's on the floor below us, and isn't as plush and elaborate as I would have imagined. There's a brown box in the corner with frames and knick-knacks, and a small bookshelf with antique books, but otherwise the walls are bare save an eScreen set to a tropical paradise. His desk has a computer with two screens side by side and a mug half filled with coffee.

"Sparse," I say as I look around.

"I'm still clearing out my grandfather's things and figuring out what I want this room to be. I actually don't spend a huge amount of time here. Mostly I'm tinkering in the labs or checking in on project developments."

He taps his eGlass and his eScreen comes to life with a woman's face. "Diedra, what's going on?" he asks.

Diedra frowns, her dark face and eyes pulling down with the effort. "Henry isn't working out, Mr. Whitman. I told you before this wasn't a fit. He's botched your pet project and is now working his way into the other labs. He's costing us time and money, and everyone here is royally fumed."

Jace pinches the bridge of his nose. "Surely this can be sorted without drastic measure?"

"I'm afraid we're past that point, sir. You're going to lose other staff if this isn't handled decisively, and soon."

The eScreen flicks off and Jace leans against his desk. "I think the hardest part of being the boss is managing people. I love the work. It's people that are hardest. I don't know how my grandfather did it for so many years."

"My father says something similar, and I'm sure I'll feel the same way when my time comes. Leading is never easy when humans are involved."

Jace laughs. "No doubt. Though non-humans can be just as troubling."

I raise an eyebrow at that, not sure what he means. Is he referring to Zeniths? "What will you do about Henry? Has he been here long?"

Jace nods. "Since I was a child. But things have changed lately, and I'm not sure how to fix it."

"That's a hard position to be in."

"What would you do, Princess?"

"Without knowing the specifics, I would say you have to consider the best interests of your company and all your employees."

"The needs of the many verses the needs of the one?"

"I suppose so. But then there are always exceptions, aren't there? People we are willing to sacrifice the greater good for. Is there a way to give him a position where he could be useful without harming your projects or irritating your employees?"

He cocks his head and thinks about it. "You know, you might just have something there. Let me think on it."

We leave his office and head down a long hallway with glass rooms on either side of us. In each room, there are projects and experiments being conducted, with scientists tinkering and tweaking. "Let me show you where I spend most of my time. This is where the magic happens. Each room is sound proof with one-way glass. We can see them, but they can't see us. It allows them to work in privacy but allows me to see what's going on and track the projects. I also have a video feed to each room set up 24/7 that I can access through my eGlass."

I'm impressed by his dedication. "Do you ever sleep?"

He chuckles. "Asks the Princess training to be a Knight?"

"Fair enough." I suppress a yawn when I think about the few minutes of sleep I had before breakfast this morning.

We pass a room where two people spar with swords. One turns transparent blue and her opponent's sword slides right through her, as if she weren't there. I gasp. "What is this?"

Jace grins, his dimple standing out as he does. "The next level in Phaser GenMod. Impressive, is it not?"

"And useful!"

I watch, mesmerized, as they do things that should not be possible. When they both phase, their swords clash, making actual contact. "How?"

"What? No guesses?"

I rub my chin, thinking. "When they're both Phased, they exist on the same plane of molecular structure?"

He nods. "Their frequency matches, in a manner of speaking."

"So they can touch," I finish. "This will be very popular in the Orders."

"I imagine it will be. But the tech's not quite there yet. We have some advanced prototypes but nothing we are ready to release to the public. But come, let me show you my latest invention. A new armor that you will love."

He's not wrong. I watch a man dressed in what looks like thin leather stand as someone else shoots him in the chest. Jace clicks a button so we can hear what happens in the room. The gunshot is loud, and I'm waiting for the man to die, but he is just knocked back. He has no bullet wound. "It's our lightest and most flexible model yet," Jace says. "Trust me, it will herald a new wave of fashion armor."

I raise an eyebrow. "Fashion armor?"

"Well, I'm still working on the name and branding, but the tests are all promising."

"Is it derived from Angel technology?" I ask.

"No. It's an original design. Most things are now."

"So why call everything A-Tech? Were your ancestors just trying to get into good standing with the Church?"

Jace shrugs his head as we continue our tour. "Perhaps. Personally, I don't see Angels as very religious. They exist. They came from somewhere. And they brought with them advanced technology. When they left, as the Church would say it, or died out, as I think is more likely, they left their relics behind. So are they some godly ambassadors? No. Advanced beings perhaps, but not godly." He chuckles. "Anyway, it's too late to change the name, now."

"Those kinds of thoughts could get you in trouble," I say quietly, remembering to consider his ideas later.

"I trust my current companion will keep my dark secrets?" he asks with a lopsided grin.

I sigh. "Of course. Your dark secrets are safe with me."

We continue, and pass a room with a table, an image of A-Tech labs hovering above. I stare, dumbfounded. "Holographics? I thought this kind of thing impossible? Can we go in there?"

Jace presses his thumb to the wall and the door slides open. I move forward, my hand reaching out. When I touch the holograph, it shifts and I find I can manipulate the angle, look inside rooms and doors, turn things around. "This is..."

"Princess—"

And then it all crashes down. I step back, looking at broken pixels on the table, glowing in green. "Oh no. I've broken it."

Jace laughs. "No, you haven't. That's the glitch we can't quite get past. It will work for a few moments, then it collapses onto itself. Someday we might have it. But we're a long way off."

"There are so many ways it could be utilized if you ever get it working," I say as we walk out.

"So true. Someday. Someday I'll crack the code."

When we reach the end of the hall, Jace turns us around, but there is another door, this one made of steel with multiple scanners on it. "What's in there?"

"That's classified," he says.

"Can I see it?"

"I'm sorry, but no. Only three people have access to that room. Myself, my head researcher Diedra—whom you met on eScreen—and your father. When you're Queen, you'll have access. Until then…" he raises his hands in apology.

We hear a crash down the hall, and Jace picks up the pace, walking quickly. Someone shouts at someone else, cursing. Jace sighs. "I should have known."

We walk into what looks like an employee break room, with chairs, a table, a small kitchen and snack machine. Diedra is standing in the flesh, her face hard with anger as she shouts at someone behind the refrigerator door.

"Henry, enough is enough. You need to stop this," she says.

"What's he done now?" Jace asks.

"See for yourself," she says, pointing to the refrigerator.

Jace pulls it all the way open, and Henry stands, covered in bits of food.

But Henry is...

Not human.

I stare, trying to sort it all out.

"I'm sorry, Master," Henry says in an electronic voice filled with human emotion. "I felt a hunger, and since I cannot eat the food of humans, I thought perhaps I could consume it some other way, but I have once again made Mistress Diedra displeased."

"Henry, I am *not* your mistress."

Henry hangs his head. He is a robot, but in the shape of a mostly humanoid creature. His eyes are large, and colored like human eyes, but his body is silver. He wears a top hat and a black tuxedo jacket, which is now covered in jelly and some kind of nut butter. There's a bit of cheese sticking out of his chest.

"Henry," Jace says sadly, "this can't go on. We have to move you."

Henry looks about to cry. Can robots cry?

"I understand Master. I have displeased everyone. I was only trying to help."

Jace lays a hand on his shoulder and escorts him out of the break room. He looks back at Deidre. "Tell everyone I'll take care of it."

She lets out a long sigh. "Thank you, Mr. Whitman."

They leave and I follow, watching their interaction. Jace treats him like a person with feelings. It's fascinating.

Jace leaves Henry in his office and walks with me to the elevator. We take it to the main floor, and he's silent for a time.

I break the silence. "Henry is a robot." Queen of the Obvious, I am.

"Yes. The first I ever built."

"*You* built him!"

Jace nods. "When I was ten. My grandfather had him working janitorial duties until he died, but I thought he could be trusted with more. I've upgraded his programming, given him more artificial intelligence and added more sophisticated coding to him, but alas, I haven't quite nailed it, have I? Henry hates working janitorial, but I fear I have no choice but to demote him."

I think on his problem, and a solution slowly unfolds in my mind. "You say you don't use your office much, right? What if you set up a desk for Henry in your office and made him your assistant? He could field messages and organize files. Minimal interaction with projects and other employees but enough responsibility that he would feel important. Create a computer backup of everything so if he messes something up you have the original files in a password protected location he can't access."

Jace grins, grabs my shoulders and leans in to kiss me on the cheek. "That's brilliant. You are brilliant. I will do that straight away."

My cheek is hot from his lips, and I blush like a fool.

Jace steps back, remembering decorum. "That was...improper. I apologize. Can I make it up to you with lunch? It's that time."

I sigh. "I honestly, truly wish I could say yes. But I have a lunch commitment with my father...and the House of Crows."

"Ah. I see..." His eyes fall, but only for a moment. He smiles again, but it doesn't reach his eyes. "Goodbye, Princess."

...

I'm running late, and I can practically see the disapproving gaze of my father as I scurry to my room to change into something befitting my rank and station for a luncheon with another royal family.

Lea is waiting for me, clothing ready, her hands nervously shaking. "We must hurry, Your Grace. Everyone is already in the dining hall."

"I know, Lea. My meeting ran long."

She helps me strip and dress into a gown. She's messing with my hair, trying to get it to behave, and I brush her away. "My hair will not follow orders today. It will be fine."

My hair is blue, with one side cropped close to my head and the other side long. My father hates it, but I love the wildness of the look, and it's very popular in certain crowds. I run a brush through it, dab some gloss on my lips and declare myself ready.

Lea frowns, but does not argue.

From the corner of my eye I spot a small package lying next to my bed. "What's that?"

She looks over and shrugs. "I do not know. It was here when I arrived."

I smile and walk over to look. It's another gift from Pip. Not an uncut diamond this time, thank goodness, but a collection of snow flowers tied with string, their white petals nearly glowing. I hold the package up to Lea. "Could you see these put in water please?"

She nods and I leave, making a mental note to sneak some treats from lunch to share with Pip later.

Darris waits for me in the hall to escort me to the luncheon. "They await you, Your Grace." He offers me his arm, and I take it and walk with him.

I'm fidgety, and he notices. "No one should be forced to do what you are doing, Your Grace."

I look up in surprise. Word of the betrothal has not been announced yet, but of course the house staff would have heard. "It's not a done deal yet." I'm still working out the specifics, but I will find a way to stop Nico Rex and save A-Tech.

He nods. "Of course, Your Grace."

When I arrive at the dining hall, everyone stands. My father, Wytt, Prince Norin and the King and Queen of Crows.

"Good of you to join us, Princess." My father doesn't look happy.

I smile charmingly. "You know how it is when business meetings run long."

He raises an eyebrow, but says nothing as we all sit. I'm placed next to the Prince of Crows of course. I take this moment to study him more closely. He's far different from the little boy I remember. He's a tall, lanky man, with long fingers and a chiseled face. He's fair, with black hair and dark eyes, which gives him a handsome but sinister look. His only real flaw is a jagged scar that runs through his right eyebrow and onto his forehead.

He nods at me, smiling, as we are served our first course, a green salad with a cream dressing.

"I trust your business meeting went well, Princess?" he asks.

"It did. Thank you." I nibble on my salad, while watching him from the corner of my eye.

"Might I inquire what you were meeting about?"

"Oh, just this and that. I'm away so much that I try to take advantage of my time here by becoming reacquainted with matters of state."

His grin falters, but he recovers quickly.

I change the subject. "That scar on your brow. How did you come by it?"

His chest puffs up ever so slightly. "In battle. Conquering the colonies in the east."

"I see." I do not find war a point of pride, but I know I'm in the minority. "Curious you chose to keep it, when we have the technology to so easily repair the skin."

"It's a badge of honor, Princess. For men of war, you see."

Right.

I don't respond, and instead focus on my food, which is now a bowl of pheasant soup. I'm sipping at it when he leans closer to me, his breath hot in my face, and reeking of garlic. "I know you do not wish to be here. But you must understand, my family and I are the only chance you and your kingdom have. King Varian has been in power too long. His nobles are growing tired of him, and are plotting against him. His inability to capture that rebel Nightfall has weakened him. And now you face attacks from a terrorist! Your enemies are preparing to strike. They see this as the perfect time to usher new leadership of their choosing. Your kingdom isn't secure, but with this alliance it could be. You need me."

I glare at him. "And you need me, Prince. You are not heir. You gain nothing from your family's name without a marriage to someone in an elevated position."

A flash of rage burns across his face, quickly replaced by a coldness that would intimidate most. "I do not wish to work with treasonous traitors. I wish to support the royal family. If your family fails, my family will be forced to align with those who overthrow you, and that is not in anyone's best interest. Together we could accomplish so much more."

He clears his throat and raises his glass. "I would like to propose a toast. Can we get refills please?"

One of the servers brought by the Crow family bustles over with a goblet of wine to pour for each of us. His hands shake as he serves the Prince, and when he reaches for my glass he spills, splashing crimson onto my gown.

I grab a cloth to wipe it up. "Worry not," I say. "I can easily get this out."

But the Prince is already on his feet, his face red with anger. "How dare you soil the Princess in this way and disgrace our family's name? Guard, remove this vile being from our presence and cut off his offending hand. Perhaps then he will learn his place."

The server's only defense is a whimper. A large man clad in armor grabs him and drags him down the hall. It is the Prince's right to do this, but it is rare, and extreme. "I will buy him from you!" I say.

The Prince looks down at me. "Why would you want a serf with a missing hand?"

"Spare his hand, and I will pay twice what he is worth."

Everyone at the table watches us. The room is silent, still, in anticipation.

The Prince acts as if he's giving my proposal consideration, but I can tell he's already decided the fate of that man. "This deal does not interest me," he says finally. "An example must be made to my staff." He narrows his eyes at me. "You are one of those liberalist pats, I see. I've heard of such, but never imagined they would be found in a family of royals."

Another serf arrives to replace my wine glass, and the Prince raises his and smiles. "Now, where was I? Oh yes. A toast. To our families. To the aligning of the crow and the raven. Two birds of prey who will devastate any who challenge them." He sits and leans in to me as everyone drinks. There is no kindness in his eyes when he speaks so only I can hear. "I will be kind and respect you. It will be a marriage of politics. We would both have a lot of freedom to do as we wish. Maybe you might even come to love me in your own time."

And from somewhere deep in the castle, I hear the screams of a man losing his hand.

PROTECT

The wind is frigid and the moon casts her long beams against the dark shadows of the forest. As a human, I wouldn't have been able to see much in this darkness, but as a Nephilim, the night is illuminated in a way I never imagined. It's not like daytime, exactly. More like everything is clearer, crisper. The shades of gray are more deeply contrasted, there is more color in the darkness than before.

Scarlett lunges at me with a sword, and I parry, our metal blades ringing against each other. We are midair, our wings extended as we train in aerial combat. Andriy Zorin hovers near us barking commands, correcting our mistakes, tsking us when we do something stupid. Scarlett is so fast, like a blur in the night. I can't keep up with her. Her attacks are lightning. Even Zorin seems impressed by her speed.

She's impossible to catch, but she has to slow down to attack me, and when she does, I push back, using all my strength and force to throw her through the sky and into a tall tree. She hits it with an oomph and rubs her shoulder in pain.

"I'm so sorry! I didn't mean to hurt you." I fly toward her, sheathing my sword, to check on her.

She grins, and Zorin chuckles. "It's all part of the training," she says. "But you are *really* strong."

She looks to Zorin with a puzzled expression. "You have speed," he says to Scarlett. "And she has strength."

He looks at me and smiles. "You might be one of the strongest Nephilim I've known. You will surpass Scarlett in strength, though she will always be harder to catch. She's...slippery."

Scarlett laughs at his word choice, and I look at the two of them. They have an easy way about them that speaks of a certain kind of intimacy. Not romantic. At least, not yet. But kindred. And it goes beyond the maker bond. Zorin turned Scarlett when she was nearly dead, after her parents were killed, but that's not all there is between them. They recognize something in the other and it draws them together.

Zorin tosses us both bows and arrows, his long black cloak, as dark as his hair, billowing behind him. "Next lesson, don't get hit."

I've had more sword training, but Scarlett knows her way with a bow. Combine that with her speed, and

I'm at a significant disadvantage. The arrows are tipped so as not to kill, but they will leave a bruise.

We each dash into the air, our wings glowing in the night, and I duck behind a tree as an arrow flies at me. It barely misses my left shoulder. I hear it thunk against a tree and fall to the ground. "Almost got me," I holler.

I aim and fire at her, but it's not even close. I'm not sure I'll ever be able to hit her this way.

The flying is exhilarating, and I relish these training moments, so different from my time with Myrddin, but equally important. I learn differently with Zorin and Scarlett. I channel different abilities, and learn new techniques only taught to Nephilim.

I inhale the sweet scent of pine and cold air and dart between trees to get closer to Scarlett. She looses another arrow and I feel it coming, and I know, in that moment, it will hit me in the shoulder.

But the arrow passes me, getting lost in the darkness, and I feel nothing. I look up in surprise.

Scarlett is across from me, a quizzical expression on her face. "I could have sworn my aim was true."

"Honestly, me too. I thought I was hit for sure. I guess I'm getting faster."

She shrugs. "Guess so."

Scarlett takes a break and sucks down a LifeForce while Zorin picks up the training. We go sword to sword. "I want to test your strength."

I push against him hard, but he is strong. So much stronger than Scarlett, or anyone else I train with. Maybe my father is stronger with all his GenMods, but I'm not sure.

But I hold my own. Mostly.

He pushes me back, and I realign, our swords clashing, parrying, stabbing.

His technique is flawless, and I can't keep up. Eventually, his sword lands against my armored back, and I fall to the ground and stay on my knees, panting and sweating and aching. "I'm beat," I admit.

Zorin lands gracefully beside me and offers a hand to help me up, which I accept. "You fought well, Princess. In fact, you fought better than I expected. You are indeed incredibly strong and gifted."

I smile, a strange kind of pride sweeping through me, but then I frown. "Is this my talent? Strength?" It doesn't seem…I don't know…enough? But maybe it is.

Zorin shakes his head. "This is just one of your natural inclinations as Nephilim. Your talent will manifest in time."

"When? Scarlett knew hers the first day she turned, before she even understood what she was."

Zorin's blue eyes penetrate me. "She was also in peril. It activated her talent. Sometimes it takes longer."

Scarlett walks over to us and slings an arm around my shoulder. "You'll find yours, Corinne. No worries.

It'll probably be something epic like shooting fire from your eyes."

Zorin snorts. "That does not even exist. Don't corrupt her mind with nonsense."

Scarlett nudges him playfully. "Don't be so serious. A girl can dream, can't she?"

"While the girl is dreaming, I must be off to do the girl's job of running the Dark Templars. You have no idea the headaches I am enduring for you to be here. The whining, the bickering, the constant neediness."

"You and TR at it again?"

He scowls at her. "I was not referring to myself. The other rebel groups you've recently adopted into our group. They are all so…annoying."

She pats his arm. "Poor, tired warrior. I'll be home soon. Tell everyone hi for me."

He narrows his eyes at her. "Indeed."

He's in the air before I can say goodbye, and she just laughs. "He's so impossible."

I grin at her. "Indeed." I hold up my sword. "Shall we?"

And so we train until morning breaks. As the sun bathes us with light, I practice the Way of Nyx, losing myself in the movements, my mind going somewhere else, somewhere long ago.

...

MANY YEARS AGO

The old storyteller stands on the makeshift stage pulled out from his carriage. He has a long walking stick carved from a Trinity Tree with its dark, medium and light woods woven into each other. Rare, that.

His voice is rich and deep as he tells tall tales of heroes long ago. I stand, enraptured. I love stories, and his are the best. His robes are draped around his slumped shoulders and his white hair falls around his withered face, leading to a long beard tied up in beads. I'm clutching my wooden sword, my knuckles white as I listen. I was on my way to practice fighting. My older brother, Kai, says I'm too young to be taken seriously yet, but I'm almost ten, and that's old enough to start train-ing. He's only three years my senior and he's already training with a real metal sword. It's dulled, but still.

I'm distracted when Wytt, my obnoxious twin, runs past me and grabs my sword, then runs away.

"Hey, get back here with that!" I give chase to him through the gardens and into the fields outside the castle.

I fall, skinning my knee and tearing a hole in my favorite pants. "Wytt, I'm going to smack you upside the head for this!"

He laughs and faces me, walking backwards as he swings my sword. "Want it back? Come get it, Princess!"

"Don't call me that!" I lunge at him but he's dodging me, running backwards like a lunatic.

And then I see it.

But it's too late.

"Wytt!"

My heart stops.

And he disappears. Falling off the cliff as he walks backwards.

I run at full speed now, no longer caring about the sword or my pants or stories told in wagons. Wytt! My Wytt!

My face is covered in tears when I reach the edge, and I nearly die from relief when I see him hanging from the ledge, his hands bleeding as he holds on for his life. The drop down is massive. And rocky. He wouldn't survive. This was full madness on his part. And mine. We are idiots.

"Hang on, Wytt. I'll get you up."

I latch my hands on to his wrists and pull, but he's heavy and I'm not that strong. Not yet. I haven't had my GenMods yet.

My arms hurt. My body is pulled forward, and I know we are both going to die. But I won't let him go. We will both live, or we will both die. Those are our only choices.

I pull again, muscles straining in my arms and chest and shoulders. I'm crying. Screaming for help.

Wytt is sobbing, but holding on tight, trying to pull himself up on my arms.

It's hopeless. I can't hang on for much longer.

And then bigger arms reach over mine and they pull Wytt up. I tumble back, shaking, crying as Wytt throws himself to the safety of earth.

Kai looms over us both, a scowl of disapproval on his face and fear in his eyes. He's shaking too. And maybe there's a tear there, though Kai never cries. Not anymore. Not since he started his training.

"What were you two doing?" He's talking loud, maybe yelling, but I don't say anything. I deserve to be yelled at. We both do. We are fools and Kai just saved our lives.

I look at Wytt, who looks at me, and we both look back at Kai and start crying.

Kai sighs and pulls us both into a massive hug. His gangly arms, which show signs of muscles, hold us too tight, but we don't protest. "What would you have done if I wasn't here to save you?"

We have no answer for him. He saved us, and we both know it, and all we can do is clutch our big brother and pray we never have to live without him.

...

I beat the dummy with the new wooden sword I swiped from the training arena. All my fear of almost losing

59

Wytt is channeled into my swings. Whack! Whack! Take that, dummy! My legs burn. Sweat drips into my eyes, burning them, but I am a warrior on a mission and I do not rest!

"You are standing wrong," a voice says from behind me. I swirl around and see the old storyteller there, his tri-colored walking stick at his side.

I scoff. "What does a storyteller know of swordplay?"

He extends his hand, and I hand him my wooden sword, curious despite myself.

He doesn't courtesy or call me Princess, which breaks some rules my tutor is always drilling into me, but wins him some points in my book.

Instead, he sets his staff aside and then duels with the dummy with moves and speed I've never seen in my life. He is a demon of vengeance, using a wooden sword like it's a Nephilim Blade.

I stand, jaw dropped, watching.

When he stops, the dummy is a shredded mess on the floor, and he hasn't even broken a sweat.

He hands the sword back to me. "I don't know, girl, what does a storyteller know of swordplay?"

He turns to leave, but I grab his robe, stopping him. He turns, his eyes amused.

"Wait."

"For what? A spoiled Princess who thinks she has nothing to learn?"

I hang my head. "No, wait for a determined girl who wants to protect those who need protection." I raise my eyes to his and hold the stare. "I need you to train me."

He chuckles, but he doesn't leave. Then he tilts his head, and seems to be listening to something only he can hear. The silence hangs heavy in the air, but I don't break it with words. I wait. Patient.

Finally, he nods. "You might be right in that, girl. You might be right."

He walks me over to another dummy in the arena. "When you lunge, use your lower body for power, not your arms. Your arms are puny, but your torso and legs have real strength. Strike from them."

I do as he says. Then I do it again. Then I do it over and over and over until I can barely walk. When I collapse to the ground, exhausted and sore, he stands from the stump he's been resting on. "That will do for today. Meet me here an hour before sunrise tomorrow for your next lesson."

He leaves, and I raise my weary body and stumble back to my room. Wytt stops me on the way, asking where I've been, but I don't tell him.

It's the first secret I ever kept from my twin. But not the last.

THE PARTY

Scarlett, Wytt and I work non-stop for two days straight preparing for the party. I have tailors come to create outfits for the three of us, and it still amuses me that Scarlett has such a hard time being pampered and wearing nice clothing.

She's squirming under the ministrations of the designer as Calla drapes silks and satins over my friend's lithe frame. Calla sighs in frustration, a needle sticking out of her teeth as she tries to pin the cloth. "You must stay still, Lady Night. This fabric is delicate."

"I *am* staying still," Scarlett argues as she glares at me with her silver blue eyes.

I just laugh. "Scarlett prefers jeans and cotton to lace and silk."

Calla wrinkles her pug nose in disdain. "That is such plebeian fabric and quite beneath you."

Scarlett looks at me like a long-suffering dog who has been denied her food for many days. "I prefer plebeian fabric," she says. "It's more comfortable."

Calla, who would never be caught dead or alive or... undead, in anything but the finest clothing, can barely contain herself at this comment. She doesn't know Scarlett's background, that she was raised as a pleb in hiding in the Kingdom of Sky and never knew her high ranking status until last summer when her parents were killed.

She just sees a beautiful patrician, friend to her King and future Queen, high ranking Initiate at Castle Vianney and likely future Templar Knight who behaves—and worse, dresses—like a scullery maid.

I find it all quite amusing.

When Calla is done torturing Scarlett, the designer packs up her bags and stands, adjusting the long, flowing pale pink gown she's wearing. Her hair is pale blonde and hangs in ringlets that glow with small Eden Fashionable jewels set to pulse with lights in bright colors. Her eyes match the sapphires in her hair and her makeup is expertly applied. Calla is always flawless, which is an art unto itself, one my friend does not care about.

I try to sooth over Calla's ruffled feelings. "I know your creations will be the highlight of the ball," I tell her.

She beams at that. "Yes, they will. Though I could have used more than two days to make three masterpieces."

"I called you because I knew only you could create a miracle in such a time frame. But if you feel it's too much, I understand. I could give Bridgette a call instead." It's a low blow, one I know will light a fire under her like nothing else. Bridgette is her sister and her biggest fashion competition in London. They have a rivalry I cannot imagine having with my own sibling, but the two of them create the most stunning Eden Fashionables in the world.

When Calla leaves, Scarlett pulls on her jeans and shirt and slumps into the loveseat in my sitting room. "I've been here less than a day and court life is already killing me," she says dramatically.

I snort. "So you don't want to come be my royal advisor full time when I become Queen?"

"I would be terrible at it," she says.

"Actually, you'd be brilliant at it, but you'd hate it."

And neither of us say the obvious problem. She couldn't be Nightfall and lead the Dark Templars from London.

"Have you found anything useful on Nico Rex yet?" I ask, while we have a moment alone.

She sighs. "No. All my hacking skills and I still can't figure out his real identity or how to find him. I hope you have a plan B in place if this fails?"

Actually, I don't. And that's a huge problem as my wedding looms closer.

...

I meet with Myrddin that night for more training. He says I've gotten sloppy, but I remind him I've been training with the best Knights in the world.

"That means nothing," he says. "They do not push you the way I push you."

Given how exhausted and sore I am after our workouts, I'd have to agree with him. With all my GenMod and Nephilim power, my old mentor can still destroy me.

I limp back to my room in the wee hours, grateful that I heal faster now and will wake up not completely ruined for the ball.

My sleep is disturbed by strange dreams of a golden raven bringing me red berries. They are poisonous and I eat one and begin to choke, but instead of dying, it is my twin who lays dead at my feet.

I wake in a cold sweat, tangled in expensive sheets that feel like chains. I rush to the washroom and splash frigid water over my face. When I look in the mirror, I am pale, and there are dark circles under my eyes. I look sick, but I know I'm healthy, physically at least. My mind feels less so.

I need to talk to Granny. Now.

I pull warm clothes on and slip out of the castle, using my Nephilim vision to follow the trail to her cottage.

As always, smoke billows from her chimney, and my skin prickles as I step over the marked stones of her entrance.

She's waiting at the door for me. Without speaking, we both sit at her table.

"It has begun," she says.

"What has begun?"

"What will be. What was. What is." She hands me tea that was already brewed and is still hot.

"Granny, please, no riddles. I need to understand. Is Wytt going to die? Is that what I saw in my dreams?"

I'm choking on my own tears now. I can't lose Kai and Wytt. I can't lose them both. I just can't. I will take him away from here, away from the Orders. We will go into hiding. Scarlett will help me, I know that. We will find a way to save him.

"I do not know the answer," Granny says. "All will depend on the course you take. So much will depend on your next steps."

I set my tea down and reach for her old hands, my eyes burning. "Tell me which steps to take. I will do anything to save him."

"Anything?" She asks, and I shudder with dread at her question.

"Anything."

"Every path has a consequence. Every choice requires a sacrifice."

"He cannot die."

"Then you must choose a different path. The one you are on will lead to your vision becoming realized."

A vice grips my chest. I can't breathe. Can't move. I'm paralyzed by this. "What path am I on, and how do I change it? Does this ball cause his death? Should I cancel it? Should we leave?"

Granny closes her eyes, breathing slowly, deeply. I still myself and work to not interrupt her. It's hard. It's never been so difficult to keep quiet.

Finally, she opens her eyes. "Finish your tea."

I know the drill, and I drink the bitter brew quickly, handing her the cup.

She studies the leaves, and her eyes are sad when she looks up. "You must see through the façade to the true threat to save your brother."

I suck in my breath. "What façade? Is Prince Norin the true threat?" It would make sense in a weird way. He takes on the persona of Nico Rex to terrorize my kingdom, then uses his family's influence to 'save us' through marriage to a Queen.

She shakes her head. "He is the enemy but not the threat."

I stand, my body on fire, my skin burning, rage boiling in me. "That doesn't make sense. Tell me what to do." I'm nearly shouting but I can't help myself.

"Have the ball. Change the course of your path, and be ready to pay the price that will be demanded of you."

"I'll pay any price to save Wytt."

She bows her head. "Time will tell."

...

I'm still shaking when I get back to my bedroom. I can't sleep, I can only pace back and forth in front of the fireplace.

When Scarlett knocks and enters my room, I turn in surprise. "Why are you awake?"

"For whatever reason you are," she says.

I frown. "What does that mean?"

"Zorin explained this to me once, but I didn't understand until recently," she says. "Because I turned you, we share a blood blond. I can sense on some level when you are in danger, or under extreme distress. Like tonight. What's going on?"

I tell her about my dream and about Granny's prophesies. Color drains from her already pale face. "We have to change this. He can't die."

"Obviously," I say, though I am so glad she's a part of this with me. I feel less alone now.

She takes a deep breath. "Come with me. We can't think when we are both so full of anxiety."

I follow her without question as she leads me outside and into the woods. When we are deep enough in to her satisfaction, she stops and unleashes her wings. They are silver and glow brightly in the darkness. Her silver blue eyes are rimmed with a silver light and her skin glows ethereally. She is beautiful. A spectre of light in the darkness.

I unleash my own wings, the ache in my shoulders feeling so good. When she launches into the air, I join her. We fly fast, reaching past the clouds, where no late night onlookers will be able to see us.

We don't talk, we just fly, letting the air carry us, and the tension begins to drain out of my body. I don't know how long we soar, but when we return to our spot in the forest, I have a new clarity and purpose. On the way back to the castle we talk about what to do next.

"Granny said Prince Norin is an enemy but not the threat? So let's stick to the original plan," Scarlett says. "We will figure out who Nico Rex really is, stop this marriage, and I'll keep an eye on Wytt. Nothing will happen to him. On my life."

I stop and face my friend. "If something does happen—and if I'm not there—I need you to promise me something."

"What?" Her face is guarded as she waits.

"Turn him, like you turned me. Don't let him die."

"I won't let him die. I swear it."

...

There is no more time to sleep. We both drain a few LifeForces, and I leave Scarlett to check in with the staff about all the party details. By that afternoon, my hair is ready, my makeup is done and I'm just waiting on Calla to bring our outfits.

She arrives late, out of breath, but holding masterpieces. "You owe me, Princess. This was nearly impossible."

I hug her and kiss her cheek. "I do owe you. Thank you. You are a genius."

She nods. "I am that."

She unveils her creations and even Scarlett gasps in amazement. "These are..."

Wytt grins. "You've left her speechless."

Calla smiles. "Then my work here is done."

It takes us each thirty minutes to get into our outfits, but it's worth it. I'm dressed in black and gold, with a golden raven on a side-shoulder cape. The bird reminds me too much of my dream, but I push it out of my mind. It's not destined to happen, it's only one possible future, and we can stop it. Wytt has matching colors to mine and looks dashing. Scarlett's gown is a pale ice blue with silver threading to match her eyes. All are Eden Fashionables with moving pieces that bring our clothing to life.

We descend the staircase to the ballroom, where it's been transformed into a winter wonderland of white and pale blue. Icicles hang from the ceiling, reflecting light through the room. Tables are covered in snow-white linen with silver threading that sparkles in the lighting. White floral arrangements are at the center of each, with white candles burning everywhere, and flickering white lights. An orchestra plays softly from the stage, filling the room with music.

The food and drink is set up and ready. And right on time the first of the guests are ushered in.

Wytt, my father, Scarlett and I stand to greet each person as they come in.

When Jace Whitman arrives, I grin more broadly than is proper.

He bows and smiles, his dimple standing out on his handsome face. "Thank you for the invitation, Princess. I hope you'll do me the honor of saving a dance this evening."

"Oh, of course."

"Thank you. I'll look for you later."

He leaves the line, and I'm flustered. My father looks down at me, his face inscrutable, as our next guest walks up.

The royal family is the last to arrive, and they do not greet us as the others do. We are sitting in high back chairs at the royal table when they are introduced to us. They are then escorted to seating befitting their ranking near my father. Norin is seated beside me, dressed in a glimmering red vest, and I avoid his gaze as much as possible.

I wonder how my father can willingly marry me to a man with such malice in his heart. Especially after what happened before.

The Queen is regal, beautiful in her own way, but cold, distant, and I see her son inherited that cruel smile from his mother. This isn't a family we should trust with alliances of any kind, I realize. But my father is shrewd, so it surprises me he thinks this is a good partnership. I wonder, not for the first time, if there's more going on than even Myrddin knows.

Jace is seated at our table, across from me. His family, though only represented by him now, is one of the highest ranking in our kingdom. If enough people in my family died, he would become King. Wytt is next to me, and leans in to whisper in my ear. "Something isn't right with these people." He speaks of the royal family. I nod and sip from my wine, draining the cup.

When Prince Norin stands and proffers his hand for a dance, I have no choice but to accept, with so many eyes on me.

I catch a sympathetic look from Scarlett as he leads me to the dance floor. Other nobles are already dancing, and we fall into step with them and the music.

Prince Norin gestures to a small group of nobles talking in low voices by the bar. "Even now, as they feast on your father's food and get drunk on his wine, they scheme against him. It's not going to be too long until you're overthrown."

"Our country will be fine, as will my father. I'll make sure of it." There is steel in my voice, but he just scoffs at me.

"Oh really? What are you going to do? You're still an Initiate. What could you possibly do to defend an entire kingdom?"

Before I can respond, the music ends and Jace cuts in, begging that promised dance from me. Prince Norin scowls at him, but I take Jace's hand and step away from the Prince.

When we are alone, I lean in to Jace. "Did you come to rescue the Princess?" I tease.

"Rescue you? Not a chance. I suspect you're more than capable of taking care of yourself. No, I needed you to rescue me." He nods his head to a group of ogling girls at one of the lesser tables. They stare at him and giggle. "I feared an ambush," he says.

I laugh. "That fear seems justified. But I think my brother is taking one for the team and coming to your rescue."

As we watch, Wytt rivets the attention of the girls onto himself, and has them swooning over him in no time.

Jace sighs melodramatically. "I owe the Prince my life."

"I'll be sure to let him know. He might just try to collect your debt, after hearing about some of the gadgets you've been working on."

A screeching sound blasts through my eGlass, and I cringe in pain and cup my ear. When I look around, I realize it's happening to everyone. The eScreens on the walls, set to winter pastoral scenes, flicker and change to a video of a man in a silver outfit and a silver mask. He stands over a body in a pool of blood. Jace startles, stepping back and grabbing my hand.

"What's going on?" I ask. "Do you know—"

"It's my head researcher, Diedra Organza. The terrorist killed her."

"Greetings, peasants," says the distorted voice on the screen. "I'm pleased to inform you I've finally found the secrets Jace Whitman has worked so hard at hiding. You can thank the late Miss Organza, though she did resist longer than I expected before spilling everything she knew."

The camera spans behind him to the A-Tech lab I toured. It is destroyed.

The camera focuses back on Nico Rex. "There were a few causalities along the way. But Jace Whitman won't be needing his labs any longer."

My stomach rolls, and Jace's face turns pale.

"You might be wondering who is next? That question will be answered shortly."

The screens go black, and the large wall adjacent to the gardens turns a translucent blue. Nico Rex steps through with two followers, all dressed in the same silver with masks.

I lean over to Jace. "You have to get out of here now. He's coming for you. There's a panel in the hall behind the red tapestry. It leads to secret tunnels under the castles. You'll be safe there."

He looks ready to resist, but I nudge him. "Go now, or you'll put everyone here at risk."

He nods and slips out behind the other guests. We are too far away for Nico Rex to notice just yet. I just pray Jace makes it out in time.

Nico commands the attention of the room. "I am here for Jace Whitman. Give him to me and no one else will be harmed."

Everyone looks around, but Jace is already gone.

Nico grabs one of the girls Wytt was flirting with. She screams and he slaps her face. "Find me Jace Whitman!"

My father steps forward, sword drawn, looking every inch the warrior even in his most elegant evening wear. "Let the girl go!"

"Here he is," Nico says with a mocking bow. "The King of Sapientia himself. A Knight of the First, even. I've been waiting to meet you."

My father points his sword at the intruder. "Surrender now or I'll cut you down where you stand."

"I think not."

My father flicks his blade and it extends into a whip. It lashes straight at Nico, but he phases, turning translucent blue, and the whip goes right through him.

The King is not a man to give up, and he continues his advances, whipping and lashing, fighting with all the precision and training he's earned over the years. But Nico stays phased...Impossible. The most he should be able to phase for is a few seconds, then he would need a recuperation period of even longer.

As my father continues slashing to no avail, Nico walks in evened steps toward him. "You see, you cannot kill me. You cannot touch me. I am invincible." He draws his sword, and it begins to vibrate and turn a pale blue. He unphases for a fraction of a second, long enough to stab my father in his side.

My father falls to the ground, clutching a bleeding wound.

I scream and run across the ballroom floor, kneeling to hold him, as Nico stands, gloating. "For all your GenMods, you are still not as strong as me. And the power you have, the power all of you have," he says, addressing the patricians and nobles, "was never meant to be yours. And someday you will return to what you were. Weak. Pathetic. Scared for your lives." He runs his blade through a marble pillar, cutting it in half, though he put no strength into the blow. There's something special about the weapon, the way it vibrates.

He holds the glowing sword to Varian's throat. "Now, tell me where Jace Whitman is."

I hold my father's shaking body as he spits blood at the terrorist.

"Very well," Nico says, standing and wiping the blood from his mask. "Grab the boy."

The two followers in silver pull Wytt from the crowd, and my heart clenches.

"Are you willing to lose your last son?" Nico asks my father.

The King in my arms is silent, and I am about to speak, when Nico looks at me. "No? Perhaps your daughter, the heir, feels differently."

He walks up to me, crouching down so we are on the same level. "Where is Jace Whitman?"

I can't let my brother die. But I can't tell him where Jace is either.

I pull a dagger from my sleeve—something I always have built into my gowns, just in case—and lunge at Nico's throat, but he phases and I miss. He unphases long enough to slap me across the face, sending me crashing against the floor.

"Pitiful," he spits. He gestures to his guards. "Kill the Prince!"

"No!" I scream at the same time Jace yells, "I'm here!" from the entrance of the corridor.

In an instant, Nico dashes over to Jace, his vibrating sword pointing forward. "You will come with me, Jace Whitman."

I can't let this happen, but I don't have much time to think of a plan. I consciously relax my body and mind. I use the Method of Loci, a technique Myrddin taught me all those years ago to 'slow time' and think things through. Around me, everything pauses, though I know it is really my mental functioning speeding up. I go through everything I know. I can't touch Nico Rex, can't kill him. But...maybe I don't have to touch him. There is another way.

I lunge to my feet and sprint forward, throwing my dagger at him. It doesn't hit him of course, but that wasn't my intention. My dagger hits his sword, which flies out of his hand, and I dash for it, grabbing the hilt.

I act fast with my new weapon, and cut through the floor around myself and Nico. I use my eGlass to send a quick message to Scarlett to take out the two enemies threatening Wytt. The floor gives way like butter to a hot knife, and with a loud crash the marble separates and we fall.

It is a long fall, with a hard landing, and I can't use my wings to hover. Too many witnesses. My breath is knocked out of me and my body aches from too many bruises and scrapes, but I'm alive.

Unfortunately, so is Nico Rex.

"What have you done?" he screams.

We are trapped in the secret tunnels, a soft glow from the ballroom above the only illumination in this dark, dank place. "By the time you escape from here, they will all be gone. Your hostages, your target. You've failed."

He roars in anger and throws himself at me. I reach for his sword, which flew across the tunnel during the fall, but he grabs it first and cuts into my arm. I fall back as he stands over me. "I thought you, Princess Corinne, would understand best of all why the patricians cannot continue to rule. After what your father allowed to happen to you."

Blood drips down my arm, the pain ruling my mind, but still his words stop me. He can't possibly know. How could he? Only a few people ever knew about what happened that night.

He turns to walk away, but I can't let him escape. I throw myself at him, trying to grab him. He phases, and I fall through him, then he unphases and kicks me in the gut. When I try to get up, he kicks me again.

I want to use my wings, to use my Nephilim powers, but I can't. He knows my real identity. There may be people above us who could see or hear. I'm trapped.

He keeps kicking, and I feel my consciousness fade, but then from somewhere, a rock hits Nico in the head. He screams and turns around, surprised.

Pip is there, holding a small pile of rocks. He doesn't speak, of course, but he grunts, angry that I'm being hurt.

No! I try to scream, to tell Pip to run, to get away, but my voice is too weak, and he is not listening. He keeps throwing his rocks as Nico turns to face him. I reach to grab him, to stop him from what I know he will do, but my hands touch nothing but air. Nico reaches Pip, who faces him with more courage than any Knight of the First. I try to run, try to throw myself between Pip and Nico's sword, but I am not fast enough.

And the blade rips into the small body.

Into the dear boy who always leaves me gifts. Into the kind soul who was ever a companion in my darkest hours.

Pip's body splits under the power of the weapon, and Nico walks away. "No," I scream, but it comes out as a whisper. "You didn't have to kill him. He was an innocent."

Nico looks at me, his voice lifeless. "There are no innocents in this world, Princess." He touches a wall. It turns a translucent blue and he walks through it, disappearing, leaving me alone in the tunnels with Pip's body.

...

There is a moment in each of our lives when we can see between the veil of life and death. When time stands still. I exist in that moment now. Pip's body lays lifeless, torn in two, blood still pumping out of him though I know his heart no longer beats. I can feel it. Hear it. Smell it.

My nails dig into the blood-stained stone, one breaking on the unforgiving rock. I don't feel it.

I feel nothing but the absence of life. The emptiness of a person who was here just a moment ago and is now gone forever.

I pull myself to the boy's body, a sob building in my chest, but it is still too buried under shock and that horrible emptiness.

When I reach him, I know he is gone, but still I try. I don't have to cut open a line into his vein, his blood is thick and heavy everywhere. He is already drained. So

I cut open my wrist and pour my life into his mouth. A tear slides down my cheek. The lone rebel of emotion that escaped the confines of my heart.

My blood does not change him. It does not make him Nephilim. It does not heal him.

He is too far dead. His body too torn apart to heal, even by whatever magic or mystery sleeps within me.

I collapse over his chest, my sob now growing power, rising up in me like a tsunami of grief and anger. It pours out of me, the tears flooding my face, flooding Pip's body, until I feel like I might drown in the blood and tears of this one horrible act.

What drives a person to kill the innocent? To take life so recklessly? So thoughtlessly?

What kind of world can create a monster like that man?

This is a world I do not wish to live in.

This is the world I must change.

It feels like a lifetime before anything in me moves. I am cold, but I do not shiver. My body frozen in the winter temperatures made colder by stone and drafts.

I feel the touch of a hand on my shoulder. The whisper of my name. "Corinne..."

I look up. They are there. Jace. Wytt. Scarlett. My friends. I know them. I see them. But I cannot move. I cannot leave Pip alone. Even though he lived his life alone in these catacombs, leaving him here now, like this, feels wrong. Feels evil. All of this feels evil.

Jace tries to help me up, but my body is stiff and doesn't want to move.

"You're freezing." He pulls off his long black trench coat and drapes it over me. I get blood on it, but he doesn't seem to mind or care. Or even notice. His face is drawn and sad. His blue eyes troubled by the vision before us.

Scarlett's face is set in ice. She is angry. Fierce. And I know I'm not just seeing my best friend, I'm seeing Nightfall. I'm glad of that. I want Nightfall now. Need her.

Wytt is at a loss. He is too tender for this world sometimes. Too sensitive and kind and wise and sweet. His face is a tale of sadness and grief that mirrors my own broken heart.

It is Jace who picks up Pip's body, piecing him back together as best he can as he leads us out of the catacombs and into the castle. Pip is small, light, but dead bodies are never easy to carry.

The dead always weigh heavier on us than the living.

THE CURE

LONG AGO

My mind drifts to the past. To days long ago when things seemed simpler, until I learned of the world's darkness. And our limits as royalty to help those we care about.

It is a balmy day with a gentle breeze as I wave from my perch in the open carriage pulled by silver horses genetically modified to look like unicorns. I'm wearing an expensive dress with beads and embroidery and lace. I've always hated wearing such things. Being a Princess can be such a bore. But lately I've begun to see the artistry in the designs, the delicate beauty in the fashioning of such clothing. This time I asked to watch as my dress was being made, and I mimicked the designer with my own fabric, trying to recreate the beauty she weaved. Mine was nothing in comparison, but it made me look at fashion in a whole new way, and I've been sketching clothing ideas for a fortnight now.

Wytt teases me about it, but Kai, who is getting bigger and more muscular by the day now that he is closing in on his fifteenth year, took the sketchbook from Wytt and studied the drawings with a serious expression. I fidgeted with the hem of my shirt waiting for him to say something. Wytt could be a turd, but Kai…Kai would set me straight one way or the other. He'd tell me if I was being silly, and he'd mean it.

When he looked up from my drawings, I sucked in my breath. He smiled. "Your fashions are going to be famous someday," he said.

I threw myself into his arms. "You really think so?"

He nodded, hugging me. "They're brilliant. Truly. Keep drawing them."

Wytt scoffed. "Princesses can't be clothing designers. You'll be an Initiate and have no time for such things soon enough."

He was right, but I didn't want to give him the satisfaction of telling him so.

Wytt nudges me out of my memory and points to something in the crowd. "That old storyteller you like so much is out there."

I strain to see, and sure enough, Myrddin has set up his carriage, entertaining the crowds that have gathered to see the royal family on parade.

I'm still sore from my last training with him, but I don't tell Wytt that. Wytt can't know about Myrddin.

That was the deal when he agreed to train me. No one must ever know. I hate keeping secrets from my twin. As annoying as he is, he's also my best friend in a way no one else can be. But I have to keep my secret or Myrddin will stop the training, and I'll never see him again. That can't happen.

I'm getting restless after another hour of slow moving carriages, and I tug on my father's coat. "Why do we have to do this?" I ask.

"We are symbols to the people of peace and prosperity. Seeing us gives them hope for their future."

"Then why don't we get off the carriages and go down there? Actually interact with them. See what their lives are really like from close-up instead of looking down at them from here."

My father purses his lips. A look he gets a lot when I ask difficult questions. Kai chuckles. "She's right dad, let's go. Give the people some real hope!"

I can tell Kai is mocking our father, which is, I think, his favorite pastime. In fairness, our father isn't always very nice to Kai. He pushes my older brother way too hard and gets angry at him for every little thing he does wrong. I think he blames Kai for not being able to save our mother when we were babies, but Kai was so little too. There was no way he could have saved her from the fall that took her life. It was an accident. No one's fault but fate.

People say I look just like her. Maybe that's why father is much nicer to me, even though I'm just as sassy as Kai.

We arrive at the end of the street, where we are meant to turn a corner and head back into the safety of the castle grounds. Instead, I act impulsively and hop off, pulling Kai with me. Wytt follows, laughing at us both, and my father, who I know is put out, joins us. He could never let us wander the streets alone.

And so we do something we've never done before. We walk through the streets of London, just the four of us. Well, the four of us and all the Inquisition guards my father has summoned to keep us safe during our 'reckless foray into the underbelly of the city.' He's so dramatic.

The street is bustling with city dwellers, a blend of plebs and pats who mix uncomfortably as they shop, window browse and take in the city sights. StreetBots buzz through the crowds, whisking away the trash and keeping the city clean. Above us, eScreens flash advertisements and news, mostly about the royal family and the parade and festival happening today. Because of the crowds, more shops are open, with booths outside in rows as shop owners sell their wares.

As we pass, people stop and gawk, but I'm used to it and can mostly ignore them now.

Kai and Wytt run ahead, despite my father's protests, and duck into a trinket shop to spend money on things they probably don't need. At a nod from the King, two Inquisition Guards break off from our entourage and follow them in. I stay with my father, because he looks a bit lost, and though I don't understand why, I feel bad for him. "What's wrong?" I ask.

"I just worry about you and your brothers," he says.

"Why? Are we in any particular danger?"

He shrugs. "You are royal, heir to the throne, there will always be somebody plotting to do you harm, my dear. It's a truth you must live with and not ignore, lest it be your undoing."

His fears seem to be founded when we hear shouting coming from down the street. A woman cries out as a man strips her shirt off and whips her back with long lashes. Our guards flank us, but I stretch to see what's happening.

She is a pleb in a blue uniform, bent over a block of wood while she receives her whipping. She does not protest, but she cries out in pain at each lash.

"Father, you must stop him!" I'm shaking with rage, and try to push past our guards to intervene, but my father pulls me back.

"We cannot involve ourselves, for her sake," he says.

"That's rubbish!"

"Listen."

I do, and I hear the man criticizing her for breaking something in the shop, something valuable. She can't replace it with her income because it's too costly. This beating is her payment.

"If we intervene," my father says, "she will lose her job, and no one will hire her out of fear of retaliation from the royal family. But if she takes this beating, she will go back to work and continue to make a living."

"We could just give her money," I argue.

He shakes his head sadly. "We cannot. If we did, everyone here would want money, and we cannot support them all. We cannot save everyone, my dear. That's the other lesson you must learn."

I bite my tongue and hold witness as the woman takes her lashes. And I vow I will prove my father wrong one day. I will find a way to save everyone.

...

NOW

There was no time to sing Pip the song of the dead, to burn his body to ash as those who loved him stood watch, for we were whisked out of the castle and into an armored luxury van.

I insisted his body be held safely until I returned.

I will be the one to sing him to the other side when this is all over. After I have sought justice for his murder.

I could not save him. My father was right. We cannot save everyone. But I will avenge him.

"I will stop Nico Rex," I say to anyone who is listening. The interior of the van is large, spacious, and lined with plush leather seats, soft carpeting underfoot, and stocked with food, liquor, and various beverages.

The sound proof glass is up, so Darris can't hear us, though he's been a trusted servant in our family for so long I don't think anyone would care if he could.

I'm sitting next to Jace, and Scarlett and Wytt are sitting side by side, staring at a chessboard, though neither of them plays.

Or maybe they are playing in their minds. I know Scarlett does that sometimes, though I have a hard time imagining Wytt doing it.

"Even father couldn't stop him," Wytt says. "You can't go after him. You'll get yourself killed."

Our father almost died today. He was taken to a secret location for treatment, and we are being sent into exile, for our own protection.

"Did we learn nothing from the two men he brought with him?" I ask, knowing the answer already.

Scarlett shakes her head. "Despite my best attempts. They know nothing."

She controlled their minds. They couldn't have kept a secret from her.

"He can be hit," I say. "Pip hit him with a rock. He's not invincible. I'll figure it out."

"What kind of sword was that?" Scarlett asks. "I've never seen anything like it." There is awe in her voice. She spent most of the semester at Castle Vianney trying to find a sword. Now she uses Kai's, who left it to her when he died.

"I made it," Jace says. "It's a prototype I'm working on. It was one of the things stolen from my labs a few weeks ago."

"Along with an experimental Phaser GenMod?" He looks up in surprise, but it wasn't hard to figure out. "No one has that kind of power," I say.

He nods. "I had just created the formula. It hadn't even been tested yet." He hangs his head, a shuck of sandy blond hair falling into his face. "I guess it worked better than we imagined."

He pauses and looks back up at me, his face pained. "I'm sorry about what happened to your friend. It's my fault. They came for me."

Before I can respond, Darris lowers the glass between him and us and says, "We have arrived."

I look out the window and see a large, sprawling estate, with ivy covered stonewalls. A villa.

. . .

Darris carries in our luggage, and I tarry outside, looking around. Inquisition Guards are stationed discreetly throughout the property. A stunning garden to the right of the villa entrance catches my eye, and I meander over to it, drawn in by the heady scent of roses and lilacs and fairy fruit. Moon flowers grow around the edges. They will blossom and glow when the sun goes down. I make a mental note to come back tonight for a late walk. The garden will be luminous.

I cross my arms over my chest and smile at Darris as he walks over. "These gardens feel so familiar," I say.

"Your mother carried you through them on many walks when you were a baby."

"Really?" I look around with new eyes, trying to remember, but I was too young. "I wonder why we never came back growing up."

Darris averts his eyes. "It's not my place to say, Your Grace. But this was a special place for your mother. After she died..."

Of course. My father couldn't bear to be here. I understand now.

I lay a hand on Darris's arm. "Shall we?"

He shows me to my room, the largest suite in the villa, and I check that all my clothes have been put away properly. There's a large fireplace, a sitting room, a huge bed, and a bathing room with scented oils.

Throughout the suite are flowers floating in bowels and vases, making the space bright and cheerful.

I'm standing on my private balcony overlooking the gardens when there's a knock at my door. "Come in."

Jace walks in and joins me on the balcony. "I could've been a stranger. A dangerous predator here to steal your virtue."

I huff at him. "My virtue is not dependent on anything that can be stolen from me, for one. And two, we are guarded heavily. I knew it would be you, Scarlett or my brother."

"Fair enough." His eyes take in the vast expanse of property as I study his profile. As if sensing my gaze, he turns to me. "I came to thank you for saving me."

I turn my eyes back to the gardens. "You're important to my father."

He turns his back to the gardens and leans against the railing, looking at me. "Is that all I am? A political asset?" There's a wry grin on his face, and I scowl at him and his obvious attempts at fishing for flattery.

"No, you're a person. I would have fought for you, whoever you had been."

"Even if I'd been a serf?"

"Even if." My voice is firm and I lock eyes with him so he knows my stance on this.

He nods. "Where did you learn to fight like that?"

"I *am* an Initiate at Castle Vianney. If you'd gone on to Knight training, you too could fight like that." Of course that's not the entire truth, and I think he knows it, but he doesn't press. I can't tell him the truth of my training with Myrddin even if he asks.

"I was about to go down to the gardens for a walk. Would you like to explore with me?" He holds out his arm and I consider refusing.

"I should stay. Plan. Figure out our next move." Which is what I've been trying to do, but my mind is scrambled, unfocused, lost in thought. Useless.

"Did I tell you how I came up with that new armor I showed you at the lab?"

I have no idea what this has to do with anything, and I shake my head impatiently.

"In a bath."

I wait, eyebrow raised.

"I was bathing, and my mind was daydreaming. I'd had the problem of how to make armor flexible but strong, and I'd nearly given up. But as I daydreamed and bathed, the solution came to me while watching bubbles."

"Bubbles?"

"Bubbles. And then it all clicked. I won't bore you with the science, but I stayed up all night and the next night until I had a prototype. And it worked."

"I'm still trying to imagine you taking bubble baths," I say, giggling.

"Really? How's that imagining going?"

I huff. "You're impossible. So anyways, what's your point with all this?"

"My point, Princess, is that sometimes when our minds are stuck on a problem, the fastest way to a solution is distraction. Relaxation. Distance from the problem at hand." He holds out his arm again, and I take it.

...

We walk through the beautiful gardens and toward a lake that glistens in the sun. Brightly colored crystals line the bottom, and I stop, watching colored fish splash through the water as their fins change color. "This is amazing," I say.

Jace nods and guides us to a bench beneath a Weeping Willow. The day is fading, and already the sky fills with the shades of sunset. We sit next to each other in companionable silence for a time, watching as the sun gives way to twilight.

After a while, I ask Jace a question that has burned in my mind. "Why does Nico Rex want you so much?"

"I'm the CEO of A-Tech." His answer is succinct, but he doesn't look at me when he says it.

"Don't lie to me. My brother almost died for you, and my friend did die for...whatever this is about." I can't blame Jace for Pip's death. That's not on him. It's on Nico. He will be the one to pay. But I need to know the whole truth of this.

"I found a cure," he says.

"For what?"

He looks at me a moment. "GenMod and Zenith abilities. It's like a ZenBlocker, but it doesn't just suppress the zen genes temporarily, it turns them off. Permanently."

The magnitude of his words hit me. His invention could change our world. Rip it apart, or save it, I'm not sure which.

"This could help Zeniths," he says. "They could be normal plebs, not exiled like they are now. And Knights who abuse their powers could be stripped of them. It could help maintain order."

"It could also destroy the patrician class," I tell him. "If pats lose GenMods, Zeniths could take over. In the wrong hands, this could topple everything."

He nods. "That's why it's so dangerous. And why it was under the strictest security. Only three people even knew about it. Me, Diedra, and your father. I don't know how Nico got it, or I didn't, until I saw him fight."

I look at him questioningly.

"He's a Stage Five Phaser. Maybe more. Something we've never seen before. He could have hidden in walls and spied on us. We would have never known."

"If he has the serum, why does he need you?"

"Our security protocol was intensive. The vial is locked with a password, and a finger print ID and retina scan set to me. If the wrong information is entered at any stage, the vial is destroyed."

"If certain people knew about this, they would kill you to prevent this serum getting out."

"I know." He looks down at his hands, studying his knuckles as he talks. "That's why it's been such a closely guarded secret."

"Can it be recreated?"

"Now that our main lab is destroyed, and my head researcher killed...It would take years for anyone else to even come close to where we got with our research. Unless they had the serum. They could study it and mass produce it in a fraction of the time."

I sigh and lean back against the bench, pulling my legs up to my chest. The Crystal Lake is still, like glass. The evening is cool, but I feel hot. The kind of heat that burns you from the inside. "We need to get it back."

"I'd die before I let the serum get into the wrong hands," he says. "I've taken precautions."

I look over at him. His jaw is locked. His eyes focused on something in the distance.

"What kind of precautions?" I ask.

He turns his head to look at me, his blue eyes intense. "I implanted a dose of cyanide into my teeth.

If I bite hard and break it, it will kill me. I will use it if I'm taken. If for some reason, I can't take the poison, I need you to do something for me."

My blood runs from hot to cold. "What?"

"I need you to kill him."

My eyes burn as I look at him. "I'd save you again," I say, reaching for his hand.

He clutches at mine like a life preserver. "But if you can't. Kill me."

STRONG

Thoughts of my conversation with Jace haunt me as I sneak into the forest. I can't kill him. I won't. There must be another way.

Myrddin waits for me, just where he promised. "You wished to meet, girl, so get on with it."

I shake my head. I had some doubts he'd be able to get past the security here, but of course Myrddin didn't find the security any trouble. "What do you know about Nico Rex?"

Myrddin begins to walk, and I scurry to keep up with him. "He wants to overthrow patricians, and given his plans and what he's accomplished thus far, he might actually succeed."

"His goals are much like the Tribunal's, are they not?"

"Yes, perhaps." Myrddin clenches his walking stick until his knuckles turn white. Hmm…Interesting.

"I've seen him fight," I say, testing my theory.

Myrddin stops and turns to look at me.

"I've only ever seen one other person fight like that."

The old man sighs and finds an old tree stump to sit on. "Yes, I trained him. Many years ago."

"Does he serve the Tribunal?"

"Not anymore. I had an academy once. I was training a group of students. He was the most skilled, but most full of hate as well. His family were serfs, and their lord slaughtered his parents and sisters when he was displeased. Nico only lived because the lord wanted him to witness it all. You see it was Nico who displeased the lord, and his punishment was to watch his family die."

The tragedy of that story hits me hard, and I sink onto the ground in front of Myrddin, my heart heavy as I continue listening.

"I tried to teach him patience, but I failed. He began to act on his own. Assassinating lesser lords, destroying Four Order safe houses, and now attacking the great families themselves. I tried to stop him years ago, along with the help of my other students. But…"

Myrddin stops. His voice is thick. I've never seen him so emotional. So torn up, and I dread what's coming next. "He killed them," Myrddin says. "He killed every one of my students…his friends…and he made me watch. He told me he wanted me to feel the cruelty he had felt, so I could understand why he acted as he did. And afterwards he burned my academy to the ground. Now, I never allow my students to know each other, so this will never happen again. Telling you about Scarlett was the exception, and only because I know you two have a path together."

There are tears in my eyes as I reach my hand out to him. His are rough, lined with age, but strong. We lock eyes. "I'm sorry," I say, though it is not enough. Words are never enough.

He clears his throat and pulls his hand away, standing as he does. "It was a long time ago. We must deal with the problem at hand."

Right then, back to business. "He has a serum that blocks GenMods and zen genes."

"I know," Myrddin says. "We tried to get to the serum before Nico, but we failed. Jace Whitman's life is in peril. You shouldn't get so close to him."

I stand and face him. "Will you kill Jace to prevent the serum from being used?"

"Not if we don't need to. The serum could prove too useful. If you can retrieve it, bring it to me."

"What plans do you have to retrieve the serum other than me?"

He looks down sadly, shaking his head. "None. Nico is too powerful. He has Stage Three Andronics and Phasing, though he seems to have found a way to make his Phasing even more powerful now. When he was a child, the Four Orders would have had him executed for his level of power. We stepped in at the right time. Saved him. Trained him."

There is a long pause before Myrddin says, "Perhaps we should not have."

And what he says clicks into place. I frown. "So Jace *will* die. That's what you're saying. It's already too late to save him."

"Some battles we cannot win."

"I refuse to accept that."

He chuckles at a joke only he knows. "You remind me so much of Scarlett. It does not surprise me you two are close."

I turn, impatient with him and his foreboding riddles, and walk way, but his words pause me.

"Stay away from Nico, Corinne. He will kill you. And you are too valuable to die this way."

Like a chess piece.

I squeeze my fists and glare at him. "No one I care for will die on my watch. You want me to live? Then make sure they live too."

. . .

I know what I must do. I search through the villa for Jace and find him in the library, reading an old leather bound book in front of the fireplace. I have the urge to sketch him, sitting there with the flames dancing against his face. I haven't drawn much since Kai died. He would be sad to know that. I will have to take up my art again when this is all over. "Jace…"

He looks up and smiles, closing the book he's holding. "Corinne, I wondered where you went."

"I needed some air, to clear my head. Our walk did help. I have a plan."

He stands and walks toward me. "That's great. What can I do?"

I grin. "So glad you asked. I need you to build me a sword."

"By sword I assume you mean a Reaver? Like the one Nico stole from my labs. The one too powerful to be out in the world right now?"

"The very one. Can you do it?"

He cocks his head, and his eyes bore into mine. "I could, yes, but why?"

"You know why, Jace. I'm going after Nico. I have to stop him."

"You can't," he says, dropping the book to the table next to us and reaching for my hand. His is warm against the cold of my skin, but he doesn't pull away. "You outmaneuvered him once, it's true, but you're not strong enough to fight him one on one. Too many have died already. I can't let you be next."

His voice cracks, and I make a decision. I squeeze his hand hard. Really hard, and I let my Nephilim powers loose. My eyes, I know, are now glowing and my wings begin to extend as I lift us both from the floor.

He is clutching me, his feet dangling, but I have him firmly in hand, because there's one gift I already have, and I plan to use it to my advantage. "I am strong enough."

...

I lower us to the ground softly, and Jace just stares, wide eyed. I wonder if I've made a mistake. I've revealed to him my most deadly secret. He could destroy my life, if he wanted. If it's ever revealed the heir to the throne is Nephilim...my family would lose everything, and I would lose my life.

Beads of sweat pop out on my forehead and I step back, regretting my recklessness. Maybe Scarlett can use her power on him to make him forget.

"Are you her?" he asks.

My brain is churning with so many worst-case scenarios I stare at him dumbly, unsure what his words mean.

"Nightfall. Are you Nightfall?"

"No."

He squints as if trying to see if I'm telling the truth. "But you know her?"

I don't answer. Because I'm a fool, and I failed to think about the risk, not just to me and my family, but to Scarlett, Zorin and the Dark Templars. To everyone.

He takes a step toward me, slowly, with palms out, like one might approach a timid wild animal. "You don't have anything to fear. You already know my secret about the serum. Certain people would kill me if you told them."

"That's true," I say, taking a deep breath. "I suppose we must both trust each other."

He grins, his dimple standing out. I honestly blame the dimple for this. "I suppose we must," he says. "Can you fly? What's your talent?"

"You seem to know a lot about Nephilim," I say, avoiding his questions.

"I've made a study of them...of you...for many years. To learn how best to use the technology we have access to. To see what is possible in GenMod."

"Like the serum."

He nods. "Do you think it was wrong? That I was wrong? To create a serum so powerful?"

"I honestly don't know."

He runs a hand through messy blond hair. "I thought it could help Zeniths. If they had the serum, they'd be cured. They would still be plebeian, but at least they wouldn't have the added burden and discrimination of being Zeniths as well. It could have ended segregation for good."

"Maybe Zeniths aren't the problem," I say. "Maybe pats are. There's nothing wrong with them that needs curing. What needs a cure is the attitude that some people are inherently better than others based on birth."

Jace cocks his head, looking at me with a strange expression. "What an interesting point of view, particularly coming from a Princess."

"I realize my rank makes my statements hypocritical. But I'm trying to change the system, in what ways I can. And help those I'm able to along the way."

He smiles. "I believe you. Now, you said you need a sword, yes? There's only one problem."

"What's that?"

"I've got a secret lab an hour from here, but to get there we'll have to shake all your guards."

I grin. "Leave that to me."

I have to use Scarlett, and I can't let Jace know I'm using Scarlett, but within the hour the guards who are paid to watch us somehow don't see as we leave, and Scarlett is the only one who knows where we are going or why.

"I hope you're not scared of heights," I tell him as we sneak into the surrounding woods.

"Why?" he asks, suddenly suspicious.

"Because I'm not walking all the way to your secret lab."

My wings extend, and I see the understanding dawn in his eyes.

I smirk. "You asked if I can fly. Want to find out?"

It's the most intimate I've been with anyone in a long time, when he wraps his arms around me, and I lift us both into the air. Our bodies are pressed together, his cheek touching mine, and I can feel his heart beating against my chest. Our breath mingles as I take us higher, flying as fast as I can as I follow Jace's directions.

We land on a large property, inside the security gates that surround it. The 'it' is an old shack that doesn't look as it if needs as much security as it has.

Jace catches his breath when we land. "Wow!"

"That's all you have to say?"

"I think that's all I can say," he says. "I'm afraid you've officially ruined me for any other woman."

I laugh and extend my hand. "Lead the way."

"Right." He looks around. "I never realized how vulnerable I was to aerial attacks. I'll need to rethink security here."

"You have a lot of people trying to break into your shack, do you?"

"I'll have you know this is a top of the line shack, with the best outhouse money can buy," he says as he leads us to the front porch.

I groan at the thought of an outhouse.

Something beeps at us as we approach. I step back, but Jace reaches for my hand. "It's all right. It's just Max."

"Who's Max?" I ask.

"I am Max," a voice says. The voice is attached to what looks like a modified StreetBot, round and rolling on wheels, but with added parts to give it eyes and attachments for arms.

"Max, this is Corinne. Corinne, this is my very first invention ever, Max. He was Henry 1.0."

I bend down to look at him. "Nice to meet you, Max."

"A pleasure, Mistress Corinne," it says in its robotic British accent. "Master Jace, I have done my best to keep the lab clean for you," the Bot says to Jace.

"You've done a great job, Max. Corinne and I will be working for a while. Could you bring us something to eat and drink?"

"Very good, Sir."

The Bot rolls away and I stand. "You had some interesting friends growing up, didn't you?"

He shrugs. "I could never talk about my family's work, and I was more interested in inventing then in playing games with kids my age. When my parents died, it was even harder to connect with other kids, so eventually my grandfather pulled me from school and got me tutors. He figured if I was going to be a recluse, I might as well get the most out of it."

"That sounds lonely."

"It wasn't so bad," he says, as he pulls open a panel by the door to reveal a very advanced retina scanner. He scans his own eyes and the door opens, revealing a modern and fully stocked lab hiding within the illusion of an abandoned shack.

"This is where I came when I was young, to tinker and invent. I was lucky I could actually make my imaginary friends real."

"Max and Henry," I say, running a hand over the silver and glass table. "So the playboy image the press has painted for you. It's a complete fabrication."

He laughs. "Definitely."

"And the women?" I ask.

He raises an eyebrow. "There haven't been any women. They were photo opps more than anything."

This pleases me more than it should.

I distract myself by looking around the lab, which is a much smaller version of his now-destroyed A-Tech lab, but no less equipped. "You have everything you need to make the sword?"

"This lab has everything I need to make anything," he assures me.

"Does it have that new armor material you were testing?" An idea is forming, and I want to see if I can make it work.

"It does. Why?"

"I'll show you when I'm done."

He gives me a quick tour, showing me where every-thing is, and I set to work on my idea while he works on the sword. Max comes in with refreshments but leaves with a grumble when neither of us stops working long enough to eat or drink.

A few hours in, Jace comes over to see what I'm doing. "You're making yourself some armor?"

I nod. "I need a disguise when I'm in Nephilim form, and what better material than your super armor?"

"I have to admit I'm impressed," he says with a dimpled smirk. "I assumed your servants made all those fancy dresses you wear."

"I assumed your servants made all those fancy inventions you sell."

"Touché," he says, and we grin at each other.

I don't know how long we work, but it is through the night and through the next day and maybe lon-ger. I know my family will be worried, but Scarlett has instructions to keep them at peace. Or at least convince them we are safe. I send her regular updates so she knows I'm not dead, and that's good enough for her.

When I finish, my fingers are sore and my back is stiff and my head aches but I am pleased. I hold up the armor, dyed golden and embroidered with a raven, for my code name Raven. I even rigged it so that my wings would look golden when I'm in Nephilim mode.

I find a place to change, and try on my armor, then slip on my matching mask. I EZ-Dye my hair blond to match, and step out to face Jace. He whistles. "Impressive. You have serious skills. You could have been a designer in another life."

My smile slips. "Kai told me the same once."

He pauses, our silence hanging in the air, with my older brother's ghost between us for that moment.

I clear my throat. "Have you finished the sword?"

"Almost."

"What's taking so long?" I tease.

He grins. "You'll see in a minute. Go eat something and find some patience, Princess."

I look at the tray of food, refreshed by Max several times, who each time grumbled that we hadn't touched it. There is a packet of LifeForce, and I suck in down, realizing how thirsty I am.

"It's finished," Jace says, a few minutes later. He hands me the blade. It is beautiful, long, golden, gleaming. The hilt has raven wings carved into it, and when I push a button, it glows pale blue, like Nico's sword.

"The blade vibrates at speeds so high it turns extremely hot, but this material can handle it, even though it's near melting point. Just don't touch it. The hilt will protect you."

"Thank you," I say, feeling its weight and doing some practice thrusts.

"That's not what took so long," he says. He turns and reaches for something, then holds out his hand. Sitting on it is a life-sized golden raven with glowing blue eyes. "He's yours. I named him Pip, in honor of your friend, but you can change that if you want. I just thought..."

He stumbles on his words, and I pick up the raven from him. The bird spreads its wings and takes flight, landing on my shoulder.

Jace smiles. "He can fly anywhere you send him, and you can synch him with your eGlass, give him commands, collect reports on what he sees, whatever you need. He can be your eyes."

"I love him," I say. "And Pip is a perfect name."

We watch as the raven flies around the building, exploring its surroundings. I test a few commands, and he responds perfectly.

"Do you have a plan for finding Nico?" Jace asks.

"We won't have to find him," I say as my bird lands on my outstretched wrist. "He'll come to us."

"Why would he do that?"

"Because we have what he wants." I look at Jace, who frowns.

"Oh right. Me."

...

I arrive back at the villa late afternoon and sneak in through the second story window. Flying is so very useful. Jace is in hiding until we enact our plan, but first I need a consult.

Scarlett is awake when I land on her patio, and she opens the glass door to let me in. "Wytt has not been happy about the silence from you," she says by way of greeting.

I hug her. "I know. Thanks for covering."

We settle into her room, and I show her my armor and sword first, because she's been dying to see it.

"Impressive! Proper superhero armor," she says.

I laugh. "Sometimes this just doesn't feel real, you know?"

"I know. Believe me. I know all too well."

I tell her why I've come. "You're the best tactician I've ever met. I have a plan, but it's dangerous and I want your advice."

So I spend the next thirty minutes telling her everything Jace and I came up with. It's insane. Mad. But it's the best I can think of. When I'm done, I exhale and slump back into my chair. "Do you approve?"

"Yes," she says. "It's something I would have thought of."

Her compliment pleases me.

"I have a few minor suggestions, if you're open?"

I nod. "Of course. That's why I'm here. Too many lives are at stake for me to hang all of this on pride and folly."

Scarlett makes her suggestions, and I send a message to Jace. We both agree the changes are brilliant. I study my best friend. She's so beautiful, fair and petite, it's deceptive. She's also so strong and has a genius gift for planning. The only person I've ever known to rival her is my father. In the end, one of them will likely kill the other, unless I kill him first.

There's a knock at her door, and I hide my armor and sword. Darris comes in and smiles when he sees me. "Dinner is served. Wytt is already downstairs waiting."

Scarlett links her arm with mine as we follow Darris downstairs. "I'm glad you're back. Let's relax tonight and enjoy some peace."

We feast on an exquisite Asian dish with exotic flavors and spices, and as dessert Darris serves us all cups of an aromatic Asian wine.

Wytt makes a poetic toast about life and family and honor and some such things, but before we drink I stand and light a candle at the empty spot at our table. "For Kai. In his honor."

There are tears in all of our eyes as we drink. But the smell of the wine makes my stomach turn, so I feign drinking and pour it into a plant beside me instead.

The servants worked so hard on this meal, I don't want to offend any of them by not partaking.

Kai's candle burns bright, and I set my cup in front of it, as I think of all the memories I will never make with the Prince of Ravens. Kai, my protector, even in his death. My mind wanders to earlier times, when Kai tried so hard to protect me from my fate.

...

LONG AGO

The ball is not my first. I am a Princess, after all. But it is by far the most grand. We are in Rome, Italy, at the Vatican of Pope Icarus. Summoned by him to attend one of the most sought-after events of the season. It is politics masked in social finery. I know this of course, but it is hard not to be wooed by the social finery.

My father has commissioned the most exquisite dress be made for me. It is purple, to match my eyes, embroidered with golden flowers that glow with their own light and change shapes as the night progresses. My long dark hair is pulled into ribbons and braids and is twisted around my head. My eyes are painted in gold, with long lashes and dark lips. When Wytt first sees me his mouth drops. Kai is the first to speak. "You look like a magical creature from fairy tales."

"And here I thought Wytt was the wordsmith," I tease.

My big brother grins and holds out his arm. "Might I have the first dance, before your night is too filled with eager men looking to court you."

I groan but accept his hand. "No one is going to court me," I say as the music begins and we swirl around the ballroom.

"Every marriageable man here is staring at you. And many already married men can't seem to avert their eyes. Watch yourself tonight. This is a strange place with a lot of unknowns."

"You are always playing protector," I tell him. "Tonight, just enjoy. We couldn't be any safer, ensconced in the Pope's very home, his honored guests."

Kai snorts. "You think too highly of him. Something about our esteemed leader rankles me."

"Kai!" I look around, hoping no one heard, and silence him with a squint of my eyes. "You mustn't talk like that. This is a huge opportunity for Father. If the Pope is impressed with him, it could mean advances in the Orders, a more prominent position, everything he's wanted."

"He's already King. How much more power does the man need?"

I sigh. It's hopeless, trying to get Kai to see eye-to-eye with our father about anything. I look around as we dance, beguiled by the fairy lights blinking their bright colors throughout the room. All the nobles dressed in their finest. So much silk and lace and Eden Fashionable designs. The food that looks more like art, designed on the tables like shows unto themselves, so beautiful I almost don't want to eat anything, but I know I will. Everything is perfect. The music, the dancing, the potential for opportunity. I am of the age of consent, though just barely at sixteen, but I have been trained since I was a child to become Queen. I know how to think of the future, to plan and strategize. Kai sees only the now, and it's part of his charm, but also why he does not fancy being King. Wytt sees the future, but cares not for its lure. But I am like my father. We see it, we know the importance of it, and most importantly, we know what to do to make our version of the future happen.

That's what this ball is about.

As the music ends, someone cuts in on Kai and asks for my hand. I look up and nearly choke on my own tongue. It's the Pope himself. Icarus. He's come down from his throne in the gallery above us to ask me to dance.

Kai frowns, but even he knows he can't deny His Holiness. I smile and nod my head with the proper respect fitting rank and station, and Icarus takes my hand. Another song begins, and I am floating across the floor with the most powerful man in the world.

As other patricians realize who is on the dance floor with them, they fall away, leaving the floor to us alone. And I truly feel like a girl in a fairytale.

The Pope is young, with flawless alabaster skin and fair hair that is pulled back into a tie. His eyes are deep blue, like endless pools of ocean, and they seem to see into my soul. "Your father has impressed me of late," he says.

I nod, not sure what to say to that.

"I see a promising future for him. For you as the future Queen."

"Thank you, Your Holiness."

He laughs, and it's musical. "Call me Icarus. Everyone here is so formal, but I am a man like any other."

"I highly doubt that," I say, before I can catch my own tongue.

I blush and he laughs again. "You're more charming than I imagined."

"I'll assume that's a compliment." By the Orders what is wrong with me? My tongue has developed a life of its own. It's one thing to sass my father, but to do it to the Pope? I'm going to ruin everything.

But the man before me seems more amused than annoyed. "I like you, Princess Corinne. You are beautiful, but under that beauty is a keen wit and intelligence. I need more people like you by my side."

I exhale, relieved I haven't offended His Holiness.

When the song stops, the Pope pulls away, and bows to me, his long white and golden robes swishing around him. "Thank you for this dance, Your Grace. It was a great honor to me."

My legs are shaking as he walks me off the dance floor and leaves me in the care of my brother as he excuses himself back to his throne. "I think I've caused quite enough tongue wagging for one night, don't you think?" He winks at me as he leaves, and Kai just glares at his back.

I nudge my brother's ribs with my elbow. "Stop it. He was a perfect gentlemen."

"Right."

Kai says nothing else about it, and the rest of the evening is a splendor of perfection. Other men dance with me, but none as charming as the Pope. Of course he is like a god in our world, and fantasies of him are just the fanciful imaginings of a star struck girl. But still, it's fun to dream.

I sip at champagne, and eat the most delightful concoctions of chocolate and fruit and breads and puddings and cheeses baked into crackers. It is nearly three in the morning when the festivities finally begin to wind down and I find a serf to escort me back to my room. I kick off my shoes and the girl assigned to me is woken to help me undress. By the time I've washed and pulled on a nightgown, I am nearly overwhelmed by exhaustion.

I don't hear the door at all, and only awaken when a hand lands on shoulder and my name is called. I wake with a start, with the fuzzy mind of someone who doesn't know whether it's day or night or how many hours have passed.

My father stands over me, still dressed in his finery. It can't be fully day yet then. He wouldn't be wearing the same thing. "What's the matter?" I ask, adrenaline kicking in when I sense his energy and see the look on his face. "Is something wrong with Wytt? Kai?"

"No, nothing like that. Your brothers are fine. It's…"

He sits on the edge of my bed, his face creased in a tight frown. "The Pope has asked me to fetch you."

"Oh." I get up and reach for my wardrobe to pull out a proper dress. "What is it he needs?"

My father rises and lays a hand on mine. "A robe will be enough. You don't need to dress for this."

"But…" I look down at my nearly translucent nightgown. "I'm…indecent."

My father averts his head and hands me my robe. He doesn't say anything, but my mind is clearing and things are starting to click in place. "Oh. I see."

"He's a very powerful man," my father says.

"Yes. He is."

"And you seemed drawn to him."

He says it more as a question, as if he needs my permission for what he is doing. As if it will make any difference whether I consent or not.

I say nothing, and I do not look at my father again that night, as he leads me to the Pope's chambers.

My father knocks on the carved golden doors and a deep voice says, "Send her in."

My throat is thick, my hands are shaking, and I can scarcely breathe as I step into the Pope's bedchamber. He is standing by a small table pouring himself a glass of wine. When he sees me, he smiles, but this time I see none of his charm or warmth. I see a predator. A monster. A god who cares little for humans.

For stupid girls like me.

The door closes behind me and the click of the lock seals my fate.

Like a trapped wild thing, I step back, impulsively. My heart is beating too fast, sending too much blood to my head. I'm dizzy.

The Pope comes closer and hands me a glass of wine. "Drink this. It will help relax you."

I look into the cup, the blood red of the liquid, as he slides his hands over my shoulders, pulling off my robe and my nightgown.

"Exquisite," he says, breathlessly.

...

The next morning I wake in my own bed, though I don't remember coming back to it. My head is pounding, my body aches in new ways and my pillow is wet from my tears.

I dress quickly for breakfast, not waiting for anyone to come help, and I meet my family in my father's chambers for tea, fruit, eggs and ham.

I still do not look into my father's eyes.

Kai stares at me for too long, then looks to my father, then back at me. And something in his face changes, and I'm sure he knows, but I can't bear to tell him, to tell anyone. When we leave Italy that day I vow to never go back. And I vow to never be used like that again, by my father or anyone else.

...

NOW

My mind returns to the present, but thoughts of Kai linger. I wish he were here now. He'd know what to do, how to guide me.

I leave right after dinner to get things in place. Scarlett will handle her part from the villa and will let me know when she is ready. I dress quickly in my gold Raven armor and fly through the night to my meeting place with Jace. We picked my castle for our final confrontation with Nico. It was evacuated after the attack and is still empty. There will be fewer casualties this way if things go wrong. Or if they go right.

Part one of our plan is already in place. I click play and send a message through all the eNetworks that Scarlett hacked, with a recording Jace made for Nico. "I can't watch more people die," he says. "Here's where you can find me. Let's end this."

Every eScreen and eGlass in my kingdom will be seeing this now. Hopefully Nico is also watching, but I'm betting that he is. This plan is costing us everything. It has to work.

I wait on the roof of the castle for Nico to arrive. I don't know what to expect, so I am on the defensive, my sword out, my robotic raven scanning the area around me as my eyes and ears.

"Pip, what do you see?"

The bird chirps and shows me his view. More trees, more rocks, more of the same.

"Keep looking."

A few minutes later the bird chirps louder and zooms in on a form in the darkness, in the gardens on the east side of the castle.

"Good job, Pip," I tell my Raven as I take flight, landing behind Nico.

He turns. "Where's Jace?" he growls through his mask.

"You won't find him," I say.

"You might want to rethink your stance," he says, pulling out his sword.

I have no more time for talk. I pull out a gun and shoot.

The bullet passes right through his body. That's fine, this was a test of his abilities, to see how quickly he can phase. Very quickly, as it turns out.

"What should I call you?" he asks with a laugh as he walks closer.

I don't answer. Instead, I do what we planned. I run. I could fly, but I need him to follow. Scarlett should be in place right now.

Nico follows me, and we are both fast, but I keep pace ahead of him, darting through the forest, back to the castle and up a flight of stairs that lead to the roof.

I try to reach Scarlett on eGlass, but she doesn't respond. Nico is closing in on me, sword out, his body phased, and I'm losing ground. I go to Plan B and whisper into my eGlass, activating the autopilot of Jace's new Golden Raven jet. It flies over us, shooting the roof around us. The explosions tear through the silent night.

Nico falters, and I expand my wings and hover as the floor beneath us crashes down.

He curses, and scrambles to make his way out of the ruins. I drop from the sky and follow him through the darkness. He heads right into our trap. I throw an EMP grenade at him, hoping to cut off his eGlass communication.

Scarlett should be in place as Nightfall, ready to sneak up on him and use her powers to control him.

I click my eGlass to contact her, but there's still no response. My heart pounds fast in my chest and my limbs shake. Where is she?

Nico turns to face me, his silver armor covered in dust and dirt. "What's wrong, Princess, can't reach your friends?"

I stop, shocked, my body frozen. How does he know I'm a Princess? "What have you done?" No one could possibly know who I am. Scarlett would never have told, and neither would Jace.

"You and your friends enjoyed a drink tonight. It was drugged, though I see you somehow avoided yours." He clicks something on his helmet and a projection beams out onto the stone walls. The EMP didn't work. His helmet and electronics still function. The video is out of focus at first, then it turns clear, and my heart stops for a beat. It's Scarlett and Wytt, unconscious and tied up.

"You have fifteen seconds to tell me the location of Jace Whitman or your friends will explode in fire and ash." The seconds tick loudly through his projection.

This wasn't part of the plan. This can't be happening. I can't let them die, but I can't give him what he wants either. It's too late.

"How do you know who I am?" I ask, trying to stall.

It works. He pauses the timer and the hall is silent for a moment.

And then he takes off his helmet, revealing black hair and a familiar face. "You see, Princess, you've known me all along."

I freeze. "Darris. But...how? Why? You've been with my family nearly all my life. And...how could it be you? Myrddin would have known."

He spits on the ground at the mention of our teacher. "That fool is blind. He spends so much time hiding in the corners, skulking in shadows, he fails to see the enemy before him. It was rarely difficult to avoid him. And it's so easy to get a new face. The Tribunal did it once before, when I was a child, to hide me from the Orders. It wasn't hard to do it again when I destroyed them." He puts his helmet back on and holds up his sword.

"Why didn't you take Jace when you were transporting us to the villa?" I ask.

He chuckles. "After the party, I realized he'd die before he'd let me have what I wanted. But, would he let others suffer in his place? I needed hostages, so I waited for the right time. Now, take me to Jace Whitman. He will unlock the serum, and I will let him go. No one else has to die."

"No!" I clench my fingers around my sword. There has to be another way.

"Very well." He resumes the timer. My brother and my best friend don't have much time left.

"I know how the patricians hurt you. What has been done to you. What your father, the King, allowed, all in the name of ambition. I have been his shadow for many years. I have seen the pain done to others. Please, Princess, let me have the serum, and I will end their rule and make this world what it should be."

The timer is nearly done. I have to decide.

"I'll take you to him."

The timer stops, and I exhale.

My legs shake as we walk deeper into the castle, into the catacombs, until we reach the correct room. I walk in first, my heart heavy at what I find. Nico pushes me aside to see what I'm staring at.

He screams. "No! What have you done?"

I look down at Jace's body on the cold floor, his throat slit from ear to ear. My voice is emotionless, empty, as I talk. "I knew no matter what happened, the serum could not be unleashed. This is not the way to save the world."

"He must still be alive! I need him!" Nico drops to Jace's side and unphases, grasping for Jace's pulse.

The moment he is of solid form, Jace's arm lashes out with a dagger.

He stabs Nico in the neck, and the man drops back, his helmet falling off as he grabs the gaping wound, his fingers covered in blood.

We found his weakness. When he materialized to touch Jace, he could be hit, but, as I watch him I realize it isn't enough. His wound isn't fatal. Jace moves toward him, his hands skimming Nico's helmet as he does, but Nico reaches for his sword and shoves it at Jace. "Surrender or your friends will die."

"No they won't," Jace says, peeling off the fake blood across his throat.

Nico grabs his helmet and yells to activate the bomb, but nothing happens.

"I designed that helmet," Jace says. "I know how to disable it."

Nico throws his helmet aside. "You'll still lose. I can still take you with me and use you to unlock the serum."

"No," Jace says. "You won't."

I look at Jace, and he locks eyes with me. "Jace, don't do it."

There are a thousand apologies in his eyes, as I see him prepare to bite down on the cyanide tablet in his mouth.

"No!" I scream, pulling out my own sword. "This won't happen. I can still stop him."

I lunge at Nico, but my blade goes through him. He parries, unphasing long enough to clash with my sword, then phases again. It's like fighting a ghost, fighting air, only this air can hit back. I can't beat him. And if I can't beat him, then Jace…

I fill with madness. With desperation. And I throw my body at Nico, sword overhead, ready to die. If he impales me with his blade, he will have to unphase, and I will kill him too. We will die together, and this will end.

Jace will live. My brother and Scarlett will live. My father will continue to rule. The world will keep spinning.

I prepare to feel his sword pierce my body.

It doesn't.

And I find myself on the other side of Nico. Shocked, I look down at myself.

I am glowing blue.

I am translucent.

I am phasing.

A buzz runs through me, an adrenaline I've never felt before. So much power. So much force.

This is my talent.

And now the real fight begins. I strike, and when Nico phases, so do I, and our swords clash. He cannot protect himself from me any longer.

His eyes are wide. Full of fear. He has never fought an opponent like me before. He has never been threatened.

I strike.

And his blade flies out of his hand. He only bested me in swords when he could phase.

"Do you surrender?" I ask.

"Never." He throws himself at me, grasping for my throat.

I grab him and unleash my wings and fly out of the castle, into the air, so high we cannot see the ground. Oxygen grows thin, and my mind grows fuzzy, but I remember, I am strong. So is he, but the sky is my domain

I twist, spin, and twirl us around until he loses his grip.

And falls.

My vision turns black, and I too fall from the sky. I hear a voice in my ear, through my eGlass. It's Jace. "Corinne! Corinne! Are you okay?"

A bird lands on my hand, cawing at me. I peel my eyes open. It's Pip! And I remember how to fly. How to breathe. Just in time, before I reach the earth, my wings extend and I hover just over the ground. Just over the dead body of Nico

I check his pulse to be sure, but he is most assuredly dead. I search his body and find a green vial. The serum. I carry it back to Jace who sits outside the castle.

I land next to him and sink to the ground. We both sit, bodies touching, and stare at the vial. He takes it from my hand, and we lock eyes.

I can read him, and he me. I nod and he punches in a code.

The wrong code.

The vial self-destructs. No one should have this power. The world isn't ready.

SONG OF THE DEAD

"**Y**ou were rash. Reckless. You could have gotten yourself killed and set us back years."

I stand my ground, arms crossed over my chest, staring my mentor in the eyes.

Myrddin's stern face crumbles into a half grin, and he tugs at his beard, a mischievous glint in his eyes. "But you did well, girl. You did well. What happened with the serum?"

"It didn't make it. The passcode was entered incorrectly and it self-destructed."

He raises an eyebrow at me. "Did it now? Hm…Did Nico do that?"

I shrug, but don't answer.

"Who can really say?" he asks. "I'll tell the Tribunal it was him. Maybe it's for the best."

He walks away, and I slump against the stone walls of the catacombs. Though some were discovered when the floor caved in, still other passages remain a secret, and our training area is still ours.

With that meeting out of the way, I jog the path back to the center of the castle and towards my father's room. When I arrive, he's lying in his four poster bed under a thick layer of crimson comforters. His room is dark. Dark woods, dark colors, serious and somber, like the man himself.

He's pale, but his eyes are clear when they open and he sees me. He sits up, his face betraying the hint of pain. "Corinne, come in."

I sit in the chair near his bed and pour him a glass of water.

After he drinks, he sets it aside and looks at me. "I'm glad you're safe. I worried about you. You were brave and fierce and will make a fine ruler someday."

"Thank you." Despite our differences, his words still matter to me.

"Corinne, about the wedding..."

My jaw clenches. I don't want to get into a fight with him here, now. Not when he is still so weak, so wounded. But—

He holds up a hand. "Hear me out before you unleash your fully justified anger on me."

I pause. Confused.

"I was wrong."

These are three words my father has never said in his entire life. King Varian, Knight of the First, is never wrong. At least not that he would ever admit. I'm stunned into silence.

"I was wrong to force you into marriage for the sake of our country and my reign. And..." his eyes grow distant as he looks away. "And I was wrong when I gave you to the Pope. I should have fought for you. I should have refused him. I should have protected you better."

My heart breaks. My eyes heat with tears. He reaches for my hand and I let him.

"You don't have to marry the Prince. It is your choice. I will respect whatever you choose. You held up your end of the bargain. You stopped the terrorist. The entire kingdom by now has heard Jace Whitman's press conference praising you and the royal family for killing Nico Rex and helping rebuild all the labs that were destroyed in his attack. We are more popular than we have ever been thanks to you."

I lean over and hug him, my tears now falling onto his shoulder. "Thank you, daddy."

He squeezes me tighter. "You made me proud. And it's your life. Your choice. As it always should have been."

I spend another hour with him, sitting by his side as we watch a show on the eScreen, then I excuse myself so he can rest. I can tell he doesn't like being bed-ridden, but I remind him the more he rests now the faster he will heal. It doesn't pacify him, but he stays in bed.

When I descend the stairs into the main hall, I am confronted by Norin, Prince of Crows, and a crowd of patrician nobles clamoring for news of my father and my impending wedding.

The Prince smiles at me, his face contorting into something he likely thinks handsome, but reminds me of an animated skeleton. "Princess, might I have a word."

He takes my elbow and pushes me gently toward the corner where we can talk with more privacy. I don't resist him, since I have something to say to him as well.

"Your father is weak, and his enemies smell blood. They are vultures waiting to strike. Our alliance must be assured, so that the Crow and the Raven can survive."

I nearly roll my eyes at him, but instead, I turn away from him and address the crowd. "The Prince, here, informs me you wish to challenge this house. That you believe my father is weak and you might seize the crown for your own glory." My words stun them all to silence. I walk through them into the center. "My father bled for you, for this kingdom, and I am the next rightful heir. If anyone here wishes to challenge the House of Ravens, do so now. Duel me. Defeat me and the crown will be yours."

Not a single one of them steps forward. "You are all cowards. You scheme and plot while my family sacrifices more than you can imagine to keep you safe and fed and contented. Get out of my house. Get away from my father. And hope I forget your faces before the King recovers. He is not one to trifle with, nor am I."

I turn and walk away, feeling free for the first time since returning to my home.

...

Wytt startles me in the hall, pulling me into the library and closing the door behind us. He has a giant grin on his face. "I cannot believe you just did that."

I can't help but match his smile. "I've been wanting to tell those bastards off for some time now. It felt good."

"Bloody hell, sis. You nailed them to the wall. I've never been so proud of you."

"Thanks. Let's hope our father feels the same way when he finds out."

Wytt leans against one of the bookshelves and crosses his arms over his chest. "You just faced off against a conniving lot of backstabbing pats vying for your throne. You can handle good ol' father. Besides, after you saved the whole bloody kingdom, I think you can do no wrong."

I sink into a plush velvet chair and prop my feet up on the ottoman before it. The fire is burning bright in the room and the flames dance across the walls and shelves and shelves of books. This was my favorite room in the castle growing up. I did homework at the desk in the corner and spent hours reading in the window nook with piles of cushions, or curled up in front of the fire. I'm glad it wasn't damaged in all the fighting. There's still a whole wing closed up as it undergoes repairs. "I'm glad you have so much confidence in me."

Wytt takes a chair across from me. "Of course I do. Kai and I agreed long ago you were the best of us three, and the one who must be crowned when the time came. We never disagreed with father's choice, at least where you were concerned."

Hearing him speak of Kai grips my heart a bit. It is still so impossible to imagine him gone. "I miss him."

Wytt's smile fades. "I do too."

We sit in silence for some time. The first we've had together since the mess with Nico Rex.

"What do you think Kai would think of all that's happened?" Wytt asks.

"What do you mean?"

He cocks his head. "Kai always believed he had to be here to protect us. Turns out, you're pretty good at that job too. Thanks, sis. For saving me."

"Kai would have never forgiven me if I'd let you die," I say. And that is the truth.

He grins. "The world is a strange place, isn't it? People we think are loyal turn out to be enemies. And our enemies, well, they might not be as bad as we all thought."

"What do you mean?"

"Did you see the footage? Nightfall made a public statement criticizing Nico Rex and his plans, saying that is not the way to peace and equality. Maybe she's not the enemy we imagined."

His voice is wistful and I want so very badly to tell him the truth about who I am and what really happened. But it's too risky. It would put his life in peril more than it already is.

"Those are dangerous thoughts to have, brother."

He smirks at me. "Don't you know, dear sister? Poets and writers, dreamers and artist, we are the most dangerous bunch of the lot."

...

It is winter in London, which means dark clouds that bring dreary, wet weather. And cold. So much cold it chills me to the bone. I pull my black cloak more tightly around my shivering body.

I expected such weather today, but am surprised by a stalwart shaft of sunlight breaking through the darkness. Its light shines on the bust sculpture of my brother, the

Prince of Ravens—his likeness chiseled into stone, but without the warmth and fire of his soul. Next to it stands an urn with what remains of his earthly body.

It rained during his private cremation in New York, and that seemed fitting. Full grief was upon us all—the wounds too fresh, too raw to see the light at the end.

But being here, in our childhood home, with his memories surrounding me, with his scent everywhere, with the echoes of his laughter haunting me, I am reminded of all that he was. All that he gave. All that I still hold of him. And so, through the grief, through the darkness, through the pain, there is a small hope. A small, but stalwart light that shines again.

I'm standing outside our family's columbarium, where all of our royal line's cremated remains are kept underground in an ornate and cavernous space of sacred silence. After this ceremony, Kai's remains will join the others.

But first, our people must be given a chance to mourn the loss of their Prince. A long line of mourners dressed in their finest black outfits spirals down the cobbled path and winds through the English gardens, so far I cannot see the end.

Wytt stands by my side and squeezes my hand before letting go. My father, the King, stands to my right, his back straight, his expression stoic. I do not know what he feels.

Farther from us, but not part of the crowd, Scarlett stands cloaked in black, her pale blond hair whipping around her face in the breeze. She lost a piece of her heart when Kai died. We all did. Maybe this last good-bye will bring a kind of closure for us all.

I will be hoarse tomorrow, unable to speak or utter a sound. For today I must do what I came here to do. I must at last sing the Song of the Dead for my brother.

I must sing it until the last memory stone is placed before his ashes.

I must sing until there is no music left in me to sing.

I must sing his soul to the next realm, wherever that might be.

There is no introduction. Formal eulogies have already been read and heard by the masses, through eScreens and eGlasses. Everyone knows why we are here. There is silence.

Until I open my mouth.

Then music comes out.

I sing in an old language. So old most do not remember the meaning of the words. But you don't have to know the words to know the soul of the song. You can feel it in the language, in the music. You can feel the magic and power.

My voice is strong and true and it carries over the wind, over the sounds of nature, over the choked-back sobs of our people.

One by one they come, leaving their memory stone and shuffling through. They don't gawk at us, as they are usually wont to do. Today they pay their respects, eyes down, hearts heavy, today they honor their Prince.

And I sing.

For hours that feel like years, I sing.

As the day wears on and the light fades, as the sun sets and twilight descends, still I sing. This would not be possible without GenMod. This might not even be possible without my Nephilim blood.

I can feel the exhaustion pooling in me like tar, sticking to me and slowing me. But I don't stop.

Not until the last mourner steps forward, memory stone in hand. I look up and our eyes lock.

Jace.

He's dressed in a long black wool trench coat, silver scarf and black suit. His blond hair is a windy mess, and his blue eyes stare into me, seeing too much.

He holds me with his look for a moment longer than decorum would permit.

I am coming to the last note of my song as he places his stone with the others.

He stands.

My note fades into the wind.

I stand tethered to the ground by force of will alone.

Jace bows his head to me, and with that gesture says so much.

A tear escapes, the first today, and I let it fall. I have sung my song. It is time I said my own goodbyes.

GOODBYE

We leave for Castle Vianney today, and it's harder than I thought it would be to say goodbye. To home, to friends—new and old—to the memories I'll be leaving behind when I climb into the jet.

My father won't be joining us right away. He has some work to do securing the kingdom and such, but Wytt, Scarlett and I have to get back and prepare for the new term.

My first visit is to Granny. I find her outside her cottage picking berries that are nearly frozen in the snow. "More tea?" I ask, walking over to her.

"These? Nah. They're for my breakfast porridge. Keeps me regular."

I snort out a laugh and help her up.

"Leaving today, I see," she says, her old bones creaking.

"Yes. I came to say goodbye."

"You came to see if I'd had any more visions that could help you and your friend."

I grin. "That too. Have you?"

She shakes her head. "You and that girl have futures shrouded in fog. It's a dangerous way to live, the path you're taking, but it will change the world, one way or another."

I hug her. "Take care of yourself, Granny. And let the staff help you more."

"Pft. I don't need anyone's help. These bones may be old, but they can manage just fine, thank you."

I leave her to her porridge and enter the castle, grabbing something from the side of my bed before I slip into the hidden walls. I haven't been in here since Pip died, but I have goodbyes to say. I thought about leaving this on Pip's memorial stone, but this seems more fitting. If his spirit lives anywhere, it would be in these catacombs. With Angel Light guiding me in pulsing blue, I make my way to the spot I'd often find my little friend. And there, in our spot, is a small brown bag.

I sink to the cold stone ground and take the bag, opening it, my eyes already filling with tears. Inside is a crude sketch of two people sitting together. It's meant to be me and Pip. His final masterpiece after all our lessons together. The paper is stained and torn on one edge, but I hold it to my chest, knowing I will frame it and cherish it always. I exchange his gift for mine, a small offering of his favorite foods, with a candle to light his way to the other side. And then, I sing the Song of the Dead. I do not sing as long as I should, but I feel that Pip knew his way around the in between places better than most, and won't need as much guidance as others to get where he needs to go.

When I'm done, I leave the candle burning and make my way deeper, into the training room Myrddin and I have used my whole life.

He is waiting there, as I knew he would be.

"You need more training," he says.

"I know."

He nods. "I'll be seeing you then. Sooner than you think, I imagine."

Riddles. Always riddles with him. "Keep an eye on Jace, will you? He's...important."

Myrddin stares into me. "To the kingdom, or to its Princess?"

I don't blush when I answer. "Both."

Myrddin nods. "I'll make sure he doesn't blow himself up in his labs. The rest is on him."

Jace is my last goodbye, and the hardest. I wish I could take him with me to New York, but his work is here and mine is there. For now. Someday...

I walk through the castle, noticing the differences. Darris is gone, and his betrayal has left a wound in our home that will take time to heal. But in his place a young man with a missing hand bustles about, doing a remarkable job of managing things with his missing limb. When he sees me, he beams a smile and bows, nearly tripping over himself. "How are you, Lan? Are you getting along well here?"

"Oh of course Your Grace. I cannot thank you enough for buying my contract and hiring me as a free-man. My family and I will forever be in your debt."

Jace helped me with this particular deal. He acted as the go between, making the Crow family believe he wanted the young man for experiments in his labs. They were more than happy to sell for that, and I relished the look on the Prince's face when he came for the last time to our home and saw Lan working for us.

Sometimes we can only do the small things to help someone, but sometimes that is enough.

Jace sits on a bench in the gardens when I find him. He smiles at me when I approach. "Princess," he says, rising and then bowing.

"Oh stop it." I swat his arm and sit next to him.

He takes my hand in his and we are both silent for a moment. We haven't spoken out loud the feelings we both know are growing, but it is time.

"New York is not so far away," he says.

"Tis true."

"And I know a guy who makes a mighty fast jet."

I laugh. "I've heard you have connections. Impressive."

He squeezes my hand. "This could work. We could make this work."

I lay my head on his shoulder. "We could."

There is snow on the ground, but it is melting. The air is crisp and my hand is only kept warm by Jace's body heat. We sit there a long time, and then I hear someone calling. It's time to go.

I lift my head and he holds my face in his hand. "I'll see you soon, Princess."

When he kisses me, it is soft, tender, with a promise of more.

"Do you want me to walk you to the jet or say our goodbyes here?"

"Here, I think. Where I can remember the scent of the winter blossoms and how you warm me against the cold."

"Very well," he says. "Goodbye. We'll talk daily, and I'll fly in weekly and we will see each other often."

I touch his cheek and smile. "That sounds perfect."

...

Scarlett and Wytt are waiting by the jet when I arrive, and there are tears in my eyes that I swipe away. I'm being so silly. I'll likely see him in a few weeks at most.

I take one last look at the castle, my home, and see myself as a child with Wytt and Kai running around the front steps, playing tag as my father admonishes us to get inside and not get our fine clothing dirty. I can still hear our laughter.

I carry that memory with me as I step onto the jet and the door closes behind me.

In life, we each must grow up and leave our childhood behind, but that doesn't mean we don't keep the parts that made us who we are.

Kai, Pip, my mother, they each added to my soul and I hold them close in my heart as I take the next step on my journey in life.

EPILOGUE

Myrddin sits in the dark cavernous cave, a fire in front of him lighting the faces of the two before him. They are called the Tribunal, and it is only ever the three of them who meet in person. They command many, orchestrate and teach, lead and quietly maneuver, each in their own ways.

Grandmaster Forrester sits on the edge of a stone, his long robes pooling on the dirt floor. He is the Grandmaster of the Templars, the Chancellor of the Four Orders, and the grandfather of Scarlett Night. He is their public face, playing all sides. "Your apprentice becomes reckless. Losing the serum just when it was nearly ours."

Myrddin bristles at his tone. "You lecture me of recklessness? What is it your granddaughter does in the shadows? At any rate, all is well. The Princess is on track. Everything is in order for her to ascend the throne in due time."

Granny Gertrude holds her walking staff and stares at him through clear eyes and a withered face. "Their

149

paths grow dark, full of mist. It will be harder to guide them."

Forrester frowns. "We must protect them. We three grow old. And they are our future."

TO BE CONTINUED

Thank you for reading.

Visit KarpovKinrade.com to sign up for our news-letter and get all the latest news.

...

Try the new USA TODAY bestselling series, Vampire Girl, and experience an exciting adventure. Available wherever ebooks are sold.

New to Nightfall? Experience a section of *House of Ravens* through the eyes of Andriy Zorin in the new novella, *Night of Nyx*.

http://karpovkinrade.com/

"I thought Nyx was gone," she says.

Zorin opens the ancient coffin, revealing

a black cloak and white mask.

"I must be him again. One last time."

ABOUT THE AUTHORS

Karpov Kinrade is the pen name for the husband and wife writing duo of USA TODAY bestselling, award-winning authors Lux Kinrade and Dmytry Karpov.

Together, they write fantasy and science fiction.

Look for more from Karpov Kinrade in the *Vampire Girl* series, *The Nightfall Chronicles* and *The Forbidden*

Trilogy. If you're looking for their suspense and romance titles, you'll now find those under Alex Lux.

They live with three little girls who think they're ninja princesses with super powers and who are also showing a propensity for telling tall tales and using the written word to weave stories of wonder and magic.

Find them at www.KarpovKinrade.com

On Twitter @KarpovKinrade

On Facebook /KarpovKinrade

And subscribe to their newsletter for special deals and up-to-date notice of new launches. www.ReadKK.com

Made in the USA
San Bernardino, CA
02 May 2017